"To think a w...
the imagination...

What put it in their...

Willie's mind reeled. "You don't believe it then?"

Violet shook her head and gave him a pitying smile. "How could I? It's hardly logical. If their father had that kind of means, would he have chosen someone like Thurman Hadlock as their guardian?" She erupted once more into peals of laughter.

"I guess that would be hard to figure, wouldn't it?" Willie attempted a grin and edged toward the porch steps. "Well, that was all I wanted to ask you. Good night."

The soft smile left Violet's lips and her stern expression returned. "Please don't try to malign the children again. You're much more likable, you know, when you don't tell stories about them."

Willie's foot slipped, and he saved himself from a fall only by twisting his body into wild contortions between the top step and the ground. Behind him he heard a soft giggle before Violet closed the door. Within minutes he had regained the solitude of his cabin and once more stretched out on the cot.

"What do You think about that, Lord?" he whispered. "She'll believe any crazy story those kids make up about me, but she doesn't recognize the truth when it up and stares her in the face. I know You created women, so You must understand them. But it sure is a tough proposition for the rest of us."

CAROL COX is a native of Arizona whose time is devoted to being a pastor's wife, home-school mom to her teenage son and young daughter, church pianist, youth worker, and 4-H leader. She loves any activity she can share with her family in addition to her own pursuits in reading, gardening, crafts, and local history. Carol and her family make their home in northern Arizona.

HEARTSONG PRESENTS

Books by Carol Cox
HP264—Journey Toward Home
HP344—The Measure of a Man
HP452—Season of Hope

Cross My Heart

Carol Cox

Heartsong Presents

To Dave, Kevin, and Kaitlyn,
the most supportive family in the world.
Your love, patience, and great ideas made this happen.

A note from the author:
I love to hear from my readers! You may correspond with me
by writing: **Carol Cox**
                              Author Relations
                              PO Box 719
                              Uhrichsville, OH 44683

ISBN 1-58660-536-4

CROSS MY HEART

Cover illustration © Gettyone.

PRINTED IN THE U.S.A.

prologue

"Are you sure you'll be all right?"

Violet Canfield laughed and patted her older sister's arm. "Rachel, you've already asked me a thousand times. And for the thousand-and-first time I'm telling you: I'll be fine."

Her sister watched her luggage being loaded into the boot of the stagecoach and frowned. "But you've never been on your own before. What if something happens?" She appealed to her husband. "Daniel, do you think we're doing the right thing?"

Daniel Moore wrapped his arm around his wife's shoulders and gave her a reassuring squeeze. "She'll be all right. We'll only be gone for three weeks, and Tucson isn't exactly the ends of the earth. If it turns out she needs us, we can come back on the next stage."

"I guess you're right," Rachel said doubtfully.

"Of course I am," Daniel said with an assurance that earned him a laugh from both women. "I need to check out those mining properties. The work is all caught up on the farm until it's time to start planting. This is the ideal time to leave."

"All right." Rachel gave in with good grace. She gave Violet a long hug and let Daniel help her up into the coach. "You take care of yourself," she called out the window. "Don't spend the whole time with your nose stuck in a book. And don't bring home any more strays!" She wagged an admonishing finger.

Violet only laughed. She turned to give Daniel his good-bye hug. "You're not worried about me, are you?" she asked him.

"Only that you're so caught up in all those tales of knights and heroes that you never give any of the flesh-and-blood

5

men around here a second look." He grinned and gave her a playful tap on the nose. "One of these days you're going to have to settle for one of us mere mortals, you know."

Violet laughed and arched her brows. "I'm not lowering my standards for anyone, Daniel Moore. Now you two go and have a wonderful time."

Daniel took his place beside Rachel. Violet waved until the stagecoach rolled out of sight. She walked back to their wagon with a light heart and climbed to the seat, a wistful smile crossing her lips. If she hurried home, she'd have plenty of time to finish *The Knights of the Round Table* before evening chores.

one

New Mexico Territory
March 1885

Creak. The wood of the windmill tower groaned under the weight of the two men perched thirty feet above the ground.

"Have you got it?"

"Almost." Willie Bradley gave another tug on the pump rod and pulled it sideways a fraction of an inch. "Can you shift that coupling a little more?"

The ranch hand strained at the metal shaft. "That's about all I can give you. Will it catch now?"

Willie tried again to mesh the pipe threads into place and shook his head. He spared a quick glance at the three men gripping the shaft at ground level. "Hank!" he yelled. "I need you to push it higher."

Hank and his helpers strained to lift the heavy piece of metal, and Willie felt the first thread lock in place. "Now twist it," he shouted. Within a few moments, he leaned back and flexed his shoulder muscles. "I'll go on down and prime the pump," he said. "Give it a few spins and let's see if we can get some water out of this thing."

The pump rod rose and fell with the rotation of the windmill's blades. A small trickle of water began to pour from the pump spout, signifying the success of their efforts.

Willie stared up at the turning vanes with satisfaction. Setting up the new windmill had given him some challenging moments, but he'd managed to get it done. One more small step along the road to gaining the cooperation of his father's ranch hands and winning their respect. . .and his father's. He enjoyed the small victory. Few of them had come his way of late.

7

He shouldered a pipe wrench and called, "That's it for today. Let's get the tools put away and head in."

"We're way ahead of you, Boss," Hank said. Willie glanced toward the men and saw them loading the last of the tools into the wagon. A hot wave of embarrassment washed over his face, and he turned away to hide his chagrin.

A hand gripped his shoulder, and he glanced up to see his brother-in-law, Adam McKenzie. "How long have you been there?"

"Long enough to know you aren't enjoying this moment as much as you have a right to."

Willie made a wry face. "It's that obvious?"

Adam shrugged. "Only because I've gone through it myself. When that itch to be your own boss takes hold of you, it's hard when things don't go the way you want them to."

Willie nodded. He appreciated Adam's understanding but hoped others wouldn't find his frustration as transparent as Adam had. Bad enough to be acknowledged as being in charge but not really accepted as the leader. It would be far worse if people knew just how much it bothered him. He watched the men ride off, then swung into his saddle, painfully aware that if his father stood in his place today, every one of them would have waited until Charles had given permission for them to leave.

"Mind if I ride along with you? I'm headed in to talk to your dad." Adam turned his mount alongside Willie's and fixed his gaze in the distance. "I guess being the boss's son isn't always the easy ride everyone thinks it is." His casual tone invited comment but didn't demand it.

"I'll say." Willie rode in silence for half a mile, then burst forth. "I'm twenty-one, Adam. By the time my father was my age, he'd been married for a year and Lizzie had been born. He'd already started a ranch back in Texas, with ten men working for him. But look at me. I've spent my life learning about cattle, but will anyone give me credit for knowing a thing?"

He snorted. "I'm nothing more than the boss's wet-behind-the-ears kid, and there isn't much chance of me ever being more than that. Not around here, anyway." He braced himself for a rebuke.

"I know." Adam's quiet comment earned him a surprised glance from Willie. "Lizzie and I have talked about it lately. We both know it must be hard to want to spread your wings and not have the opportunity to do it."

"It's not like anyone's trying to hold me down," Willie said. "I know Pa doesn't set out to undermine me; neither does Uncle Jeff. They don't have to. All the hands who've worked for us for years just look to them for direction as a matter of course. When I try to see it from their point of view, I know that to them, I'm still the little kid who put a whole bottle of pepper sauce in the bunkhouse beans. Why should they take orders from me?"

Adam took his time before replying. "What would you think about coming in with me as a partner?" He grinned at Willie's look of astonishment.

"Think about it. You're good with livestock. Like you said, you've been learning about them all your life. It would give you a chance to have something of your own and more say in what goes on. What do you think?"

Willie swallowed hard and scanned the distant horizon. Maybe Adam would assume his silence indicated deep thought instead of a struggle with emotions that threatened to choke him. The knowledge that his sister's husband thought enough of him to open up an opportunity like this meant more to him than Adam could dream.

"I appreciate it," he said in a voice rough with suppressed feeling. "But it still wouldn't be like being out on my own. I need a chance to find out what I can do. You're good with horses, Adam. You have a gift for taking a broomtail and turning it into a good cow horse. You went with the gift you've been given and proved yourself. But I'm a cattleman; always have been, always will be. I'd love to have my own say on my own spread." He set his jaw. "But I don't guess that's likely to happen."

He shot a sideways glance at his brother-in-law. "I hope

you know I appreciate the offer."

Adam nodded. "I understand. That's how I felt a few years ago, when I worked for your dad and uncle. I couldn't have asked for better men to work for, but I wanted my own place so bad it just about twisted me apart inside."

"That's how it is with me," Willie agreed, grateful for the opportunity to share the dream that had gnawed at him for so long. "I don't want to sound ungrateful; I just want to find out what I can do on my own."

They topped a rise, and the ranch buildings came into view. Willie pulled his mount to a stop and squinted into the sun. "Is that a buggy parked in front of the house?" he asked, more to himself than to Adam. "Mother didn't say anything about having company. Wonder who it is?" The two men touched their horses' flanks with their heels and rode toward the house at a trot.

A cozy scene greeted them when they stepped onto the front porch after tending to their horses. Willie's parents, Charles and Abby, sat in matching rocking chairs facing a man Willie didn't recognize. Three towheaded children sat quietly nearby.

Abby sprang to her feet with a glad cry when Willie approached. "You'll never guess who's here!" She laid one hand on Willie's arm and held the other out to indicate their dignified-looking visitor. "Do you remember my cousin, Lewis Monroe? You were just a little boy the last time you saw him."

The older gentleman stood and clasped Willie's outstretched hand in a damp grip that made Willie want to wipe his palm on his pants leg. He had only foggy memories of his visit to his mother's childhood home in Virginia and none at all of Lewis Monroe.

"And this is my son-in-law, Adam McKenzie," Abby continued. "He and Lizzie have been married four and a half years now, and their horse ranch adjoins our property on the northwest."

"Finest horses anywhere in this territory," Charles put in, giving Adam an approving nod. "He's done a good job of building his place from scratch."

Willie tried to stifle the spasm of envy at Charles's evident pride in Adam's accomplishments. What wouldn't he give to have his father speak of him in the same admiring tone!

Lewis Monroe shook hands with Adam and remained standing, smoothing his salt-and-pepper hair into place. "I was just explaining the purpose of my visit to Charles and Cousin Abby," he said. "I am an attorney, and I have fallen heir to a most unpleasant duty on behalf of a longtime client, now deceased."

He waved the three youngsters to their feet with an imperious gesture. "The mother of these children departed this mortal coil several years ago. Sadly, their father also passed on quite recently. In his last will and testament, he named a lifelong friend as their guardian, a man whose whereabouts I found it extremely difficult to trace." A peevish expression flickered across his face, then was gone.

"After making diligent inquiries, I ascertained that the gentleman in question currently resides in Arizona Territory. Accordingly, I am accompanying these little orphans to their new home." He paused and bowed his head, as if awaiting some sort of accolade.

"Do they have names?" Willie's outburst surprised even him. He knew better than to do anything that would violate his mother's code of hospitality. At the same time, the way Monroe pointedly ignored the youngsters rankled. Willie knew all too well how it felt to be overlooked.

Monroe looked up with an expression that told Willie he didn't appreciate the lack of regard for his tale of self-sacrifice. Nevertheless, he turned to the silent children and pointed them out one by one.

"The Wingates," he announced. "Frederick, age ten; Jessica, age seven; and Tobias, age five."

"Toby," the small boy corrected, then lapsed into silence.

The other children didn't speak but focused hostile gazes on Monroe. Willie couldn't blame them. The lawyer obviously resented the intrusion of their father's death into his neatly-ordered existence. In the same circumstances, he wouldn't be Willie's favorite person, either.

"As I was saying before you rode up," Monroe continued with a sniff, "it has been so many years since I'd seen dear Cousin Abby, I decided to break our journey and take a brief respite from the train."

"And I've asked him to stay with us for a couple of days to rest up before they continue their trip," Abby put in with a fond glance toward her cousin and his young charges. "It will be such a delight to hear children's voices in this house again.

"Speaking of children. . ." She turned her gaze to Adam. "How is Lizzie?"

"Tired a lot of the time, but Doc says that's to be expected," Adam answered with a grin. "She's about ready for the waiting to be over."

"Aren't we all!" Abby laughed. "We hadn't gotten to that bit of news yet, Lewis. I'm going to become a grandmother in just a couple of months."

"What delightful news! Children are a blessing." He cast a swift glance at the three young Wingates and cleared his throat. "My heartiest congratulations," he added in a more subdued tone.

"Yep. In a couple more months, I'll be married to an old grandma," Charles quipped, earning an outraged sputter from his wife. He turned his attention to Willie. "How's the windmill coming, Son?"

"We pumped water today. It's ready to be plumbed to the tank. I'll get the men on it first thing in the morning."

Charles waved his hand. "Hank can see to that. You're going to be busy riding herd on these three." He nodded at the children huddled near Monroe.

Willie turned to his mother in disbelief. She smiled and nodded gently. "Yes, Dear. Your father has to meet with some of the territorial legislators tomorrow, and I'll be catching up on family news with Cousin Lewis. I'm sure these little ones would much rather have you show them the ranch than sit around listening to us reminisce. You won't mind, will you?"

A fist to the stomach couldn't have knocked the wind out of Willie more effectively. Hard as he tried, he couldn't get anyone around here to take him seriously. He'd overseen the windmill, felt immense pride at its imminent completion. Now the ranch hands would finish it without any need of his help, since he'd been elected as the first choice for a nursemaid. He clenched his teeth so tightly his jaw ached.

Watching kids, of all things! Just the thing to prove his worth. A quick glance at the three little orphans showed him they studied him with about as much enthusiasm as he felt toward them. The realization caught him up short. At least he still had a father and mother and the hope of future opportunities to win their approval. These youngsters had nothing left but memories. What would a couple of days brightening their lives matter?

He slanted a look at Monroe and made his decision. Time spent in the stuffy lawyer's company would be enough to try the patience of anyone, much less a child who'd lost both parents and wound up being foisted off on a total stranger. Giving them a chance to see the West through the eyes of someone who knew and loved it would be the best preparation they could have for a smooth start to their new life. Besides, it might even be fun.

"Not at all." He returned his mother's smile. "I'll be happy to show them around."

two

"Williiee!" Jessica's plaintive voice set every nerve in his body jangling.

Willie winced and turned around, hoping the smile plastered on his face looked friendly. How could one little girl produce such a shrill tone? And one with so much volume? He noted the sun's position, almost straight overhead. Had he only had charge of these youngsters for one short morning?

"What is it?" he asked, trying to keep his voice even. At least he could count on his family's company during lunch. Adult conversation had never looked more appealing.

"My bonnet blew off. It's caught in the top of that tree!" China blue eyes puddled with tears.

Willie craned his neck to view the uppermost branches of the stately cottonwood. The bonnet dangled by one string, flapping in the spring breeze like a billowing flag. *Not quite at the top,* he consoled himself. *Maybe only forty feet or so up there.*

He looked down at Jessica again. Both brothers now flanked her on either side, and they each rested a hand on one of her shoulders. Three solemn pairs of eyes stared at him without blinking.

He sighed, accepting the inevitable. "All right, I'll go up and get it." He gripped either side of the broad trunk with his boots and tried to shinny up to the lowest branch. The slick leather soles gave him no purchase, and he slid down faster than he could climb. Muttering, he pulled the boots off and set them at the base of the tree.

His socks would never be fit to wear again after this climb. Willie felt the cottonwood's rough bark snag the knitted fabric and poke at his tender insteps. He gritted his teeth and inched

14

his way upward, determined to retrieve the bonnet. No one would be able to say Willie Bradley couldn't even nursemaid a bunch of babies.

Having reached the first branch, his climb became easier. He moved from limb to limb, testing the ever-smaller branches before trusting them with his weight. At last he reached the level of the bonnet. Wrapping one arm securely around the trunk, he stretched the other out to its fullest extent. The bonnet dangled out of reach.

Willie glanced toward the ground, where Jessica looked up at him with trusting eyes. "Don't you have another bonnet?" he called. She shook her head violently. Even from his present height he could see her chin tremble.

Calling himself every kind of idiot, he released his hold on the trunk and eased himself along the branch, trying not to envision the path he'd take through those projecting limbs if he lost his grip and plunged to earth. The branch dipped precariously, and Willie froze until it stopped swaying. Not even daring to breathe, he extended his arm with infinite care and snagged the elusive bonnet with the tips of his fingers.

Going down didn't take nearly as much time as the climb up. Willie maneuvered his way to increasingly larger branches, reaching the lowermost limb at last and then sliding the rest of the way down the trunk. His abused feet protested when he hit the ground, and he had to force himself not to flinch. He handed the bonnet to Jessica with a flourish.

"Thank you." She flashed a dimpled smile and tied the strings into a prim bow under her chin.

That smile made him feel like he had when water streamed from the windmill. He patted her on the head and picked his way over to his boots, closing his eyes with relief when his foot slid into the protection of the sturdy leather sole. He stepped into the other boot.

"Yeoww!" A sharp pain shot through the sole of his foot. Willie flung the boot on the ground and grabbed the injured member with both hands, hopping around on his good foot, all the while wondering how long it took for a scorpion sting to render its victim incapable of walking.

When the pain subsided somewhat, he picked up his boot and carefully upended it. A jagged chunk of obsidian rolled out and landed at his feet. Willie picked it up and studied it. Unless it had developed the ability to jump, he didn't see how it could have landed in his upright boot on its own.

He jammed his foot back into the boot. Ignoring the throbbing pain, he stood over the children. He balled his hands into fists. "How did that rock get in there?" he demanded.

Three innocent faces turned upward to meet his outraged glare. "We don't know," Frederick said. "Do we?" He looked at his brother and sister for confirmation. Three blond heads wagged back and forth in solemn denial.

"Cross my heart," Toby affirmed.

Willie gritted his teeth and turned back toward the ranch buildings. It wouldn't take more than ten minutes to get back there at a slow limp. No point in pressing this issue. They'd only be around another day and a half.

A giggle stopped him in midstride. He whirled, ready to pounce on the offender and wring out a confession. Three guileless pairs of eyes met his angry gaze. "All right," he began, "which one of you—"

The clanging of the dinner bell broke into his tirade, and the children scampered off with squeals of delight. Willie limped along behind them, deep in thought.

❧

That night he lay in bed with his lamp turned low and studied the dancing shadows on the ceiling. Scattered thoughts flitted through his mind, changing as quickly as the dark shapes on the plaster overhead.

He'd always considered himself a fairly patient man, but not anymore. Not after today. Only twelve hours spent in the company of the Wingate children had completely altered his perception of himself. He turned down the lamp wick until the tiny flame went out and rolled over on his side.

It didn't make sense. He'd spent plenty of time around his uncle Jeff's kids, and they'd never produced this reaction. And goodness knew, Jeff and Judith's four offspring had enough feistiness to make every ranch hand on the place go into hiding whenever they came around.

Lizzie's baby was due to come along in just a few more weeks. The idea of being an uncle had thrilled him. . .up to now. Maybe he just couldn't take a joke.

No, he couldn't accept that idea. He and Lizzie had pulled more than their share of ornery pranks in their day. He understood the need for kids to let off some steam. He accepted that as part of growing up. But these kids. . . .

What was it about them that got under his skin so? He couldn't put his finger on it. In fact, he hadn't caught them doing anything outright. He had his suspicions, though, and plenty of them. That rock in his boot, for instance. Looking back, the whole episode of the bonnet in the tree didn't ring true—no matter how many times they crossed their hearts and proclaimed their innocence. The breeze hadn't been all that strong, after all.

If only he could catch them in the act. Those cherubic faces didn't line up with the tricks Willie felt sure they'd pulled. To look at them, a body would think they were the embodiment of innocence. In their case, though, Willie had the uneasy feeling that innocence might only run skin deep.

The strain of the day took its toll and his eyelids drifted shut. One more day. Just one more morning and afternoon with them. In the evening, they'd be busy packing; and by the following morning, they'd be safely on their way to Arizona Territory and their new guardian. *And may the Lord have mercy on his soul.*

&

How many ways could three little kids find to aggravate a person beyond endurance? If many more existed than what the Wingates had already dished out that day, Willie didn't want to know about them.

And the worst of it wasn't even the things they came up with to antagonize him, but the fact that no one but him seemed to be aware of it. Unless. . .Lewis Monroe's odd behavior puzzled Willie. The way he skittered away with a furtive look in his eye every time they came near made Willie wonder just how much the man had endured on the trip west. Maybe he had good reason for keeping them at arm's length.

When he'd voiced that thought to his father, though, Charles only laughed.

"Seems to me I remember you playing a prank or two yourself," he reminded Willie, clapping him on the shoulder.

Twice that morning, Willie appealed to his mother, only to be admonished about the need to show kindness to three little waifs whose lives had been turned upside down. "Really, Son, you must have a little patience. Think how upset and frightened those poor little orphans must be. This is your opportunity to set a good example and plant some seeds of kindness."

Willie stared at her, goggle-eyed. What had happened to the woman who'd been able to spot every one of his misdeeds while he was growing up? Granted, she'd been in a dreamy state about children ever since Lizzie and Adam announced their forthcoming new arrival. *Even so, you'd think she'd be able to see past that angelic front of theirs.*

"Patience," he muttered. "I'll show them 'patience' if they try to set me up again." So far that day, he'd survived a loose cinch when he saddled up the horses to give the kids a ride and a pile of hay "accidentally" knocked down from the loft when he walked underneath—he had tolerated those with fairly good grace. He hadn't even given them the satisfaction of losing his temper over the salt in his coffee at lunch. But when he encountered—painfully—the gravel on the outhouse seat, his long-suffering reached its limit.

Afterward, he couldn't remember everything he'd said to the kids. He only knew that whatever it was, it seemed to put the fear in them. All afternoon, they behaved more like normal children than ever before. Willie's good nature reasserted itself. As long as they chose to cooperate, he would meet them halfway. He could be friendly and still maintain a degree of caution.

His resolve lasted throughout the remainder of the afternoon and into the evening. *Just another hour,* he congratulated himself, *and they'll be getting ready for bed. In the morning they'll be gone.* He walked down the hall, whistling a cheerful tune.

Frederick approached him with a serious expression. "Could you help me with something?"

Willie fixed the youngster with a suspicious gaze. "What do you need?"

The boy's forehead creased in a frown. "I heard somebody say it couldn't be done. I think they're wrong, and I'd like you to help me prove it. Would you?"

"Depends." Willie shifted from one foot to the other, his uneasiness growing. "What exactly do you want to prove?"

Frederick's face blossomed into a smile, seeming to take Willie's response for acquiescence. "It's about physical coordination. You're able to do so many things that it ought to be easy. Come on."

He led the way a short distance down the hallway to the door of Willie's bedroom and swung it open. "Now you stand behind the door and stick two fingers through the crack, like this. Good, there's just enough room for you to get your fingers through. I'll go stand on the other side." He suited action to his words, then produced an egg from his jacket pocket and balanced it on Willie's outstretched fingers.

"Hey!" Willie protested.

"I'll take the egg from you," Frederick continued, slipping his fingers through Willie's, "and slide it a couple of inches higher. Then you bring your fingers up to mine, and we'll take turns moving it up. See?"

"Like this?" Willie maneuvered his fingers through the crack and successfully retrieved the egg. "And what's this supposed to prove?"

"I heard Mr. Monroe say he'd read an article that said most people didn't have the coordination to do this. But I think he's wrong." The boy slid the egg a notch higher, his face a study in concentration.

"Seems simple enough to me," Willie agreed, getting into the spirit of the endeavor. "Looks like it just takes a good eye and a steady hand." He eased his fingers between Frederick's and moved the egg up an inch.

"That's what I thought." Frederick nodded solemnly. "I knew you'd be good at this." His fingertips touched Willie's, then moved back just out of reach. "What's that?"

"What's what?" Focused on maintaining the egg's delicate balance, Willie gave him scant attention.

Frederick craned his neck and cupped a hand to his ear in a dramatic gesture. "Someone's calling. I think it's your mother. I'll go see." He sprinted off down the hallway and rounded the corner toward the parlor.

"Wait a minute! What about the egg?" Only the sound of Frederick's retreating footsteps met his ears. "Frederick!" he bellowed.

Silence.

The truth dawned. "I've been had by a ten year old! Wait'll I get my hands on that little guttersnipe." He peered through the crack and studied the egg, which had begun to wobble. "Easy now. Easy," he told himself. There had to be a way to lower it to the ground without breaking it. Holding his breath, Willie tilted his fingers every so slightly back toward the door and bent his knees, inching toward the floor.

True to his expectations, bracing the egg against the door gave it the added stability it needed to follow his fingers smoothly along the groove between the door and the frame. Willie grinned. "Thought he could put one over on me, did he?" he gloated. Little did young Frederick know he'd pitted his wits against those of an expert jokester. With a triumphant grin, Willie slid lower until one knee rested on the floor. . .and his fingers met the top of the lower hinge.

He stared a moment, then slipped the fingers of his other hand below the hinge. No good. He'd never be able to drop the egg, then catch it again. Maybe. . .he stretched his arm out, then groaned when he realized he couldn't reach completely around the door.

"Frederick?" he called again. "Jessica? Toby? *Anyone?*" With a sigh, Willie accepted the inevitable and withdrew his cramped fingers. The egg splatted on the floor.

He poured water from the pitcher on his dresser into the basin and grabbed an old shirt to clean up the slimy mess, his ire mounting higher with every swipe.

"Little sneak. Rotten little coyote." Willie stormed down the hallway and burst into the parlor. The gathering there looked the picture of domestic tranquility. Charles leaned back contentedly in his armchair, while Abby stitched a nightdress for the coming grandchild. Frederick, Jessica, and Toby sprawled on the rug, looking at a picture book, while Lewis Monroe eyed them with a wariness Willie recognized all too well.

"You." His pointing finger quivered in the direction of Frederick's nose. "Did you really think you could get away with that?"

"Sir?" Frederick looked up, his face registering puzzled innocence.

"Willie, what are you going on about?" Abby set her sewing aside and leaned forward in her chair.

"The little wretch set me up. Gave me an egg to hold from behind the door, then went chasing off and left me standing there. I just now finished cleaning up the mess."

Abby's brow knitted in confusion. "Why would you stand behind a door with an egg, Dear? And why blame Frederick if you dropped it?"

Willie opened his mouth to speak, but the words caught in his throat. He'd been set up. . .again. No one would take his word against that of a "poor little orphan," with the possible exception of Lewis Monroe, who gazed at him with an air of commiseration. He turned on his heel and strode from the room. They'd be gone early tomorrow. If he could just hold out a few hours more, his troubles would be over and life could get back to normal.

three

"Look at them. Have you ever seen such little cherubs?"

Willie stared at his mother in disbelief. After living through all the havoc he and Lizzie had created during their growing-up years, how could she be fooled by a pair of blue eyes? Three pairs, he amended, turning to examine the Wingate children, who stood next to the waiting wagon. He had to admit they put on a good act, and he should know—he'd mustered up that same guileless mien a good many times in his day. But on his best day, he'd never achieved that degree of polished perfection.

His mother had a point. *Cherubic* seemed the only way to describe the faces staring back at him. To look at them now, scrubbed and fresh in the early morning sunlight, one would never think those sweet-looking angels could devise such devilish schemes. He had to acknowledge mastery when he saw it.

"Good-bye, my dears." Abby gathered first Jessica, then the two boys in a warm hug. "May you have a safe trip and find a warm, happy home waiting for you at journey's end." She turned to Willie. "What's keeping your father and Cousin Lewis?"

"I'll go see," he volunteered, relieved at the opportunity to get away. He hurried into the house and collided with Charles just inside the doorway.

"Get Hank," his father ordered. "I need to send him for the doctor." He drew a deep breath. "Lewis seems to have broken his leg." A pitiful moan came from farther down the hallway.

"How'd it happen?" Willie asked, trying to fight down his rising suspicion. The kids had been standing outside for a good twenty minutes. Surely they couldn't have had anything to do with it.

"He must have tripped over his valise. But that isn't important
23

right now. Just get Hank on his way!" Charles turned back to the stricken lawyer, calling for Abby as he went.

The next few hours remained a blur in Willie's memory. He helped his father lift the groaning man and carry him to bed, fetched items his mother called for, and grudgingly watched over the Wingate children until the doctor arrived and Abby felt free to leave her cousin's side.

"Poor Lewis," she sighed. "He's in such pain, and it's making him terribly agitated. He seems convinced that someone tied a string across the bottom of his doorway. I tried to tell him that was impossible. He must have fallen over his valise. I went out into the hallway a few moments ago and checked just to reassure him. Of course there was no string there, but he keeps insisting on it."

Her voice took on a tender note. "He takes his responsibility to those children so seriously. Even in his pain, he keeps calling their names." She shook her head. "I'd better go tell the poor little things their trip will have to be delayed."

Willie flinched. Having the Wingates underfoot any longer than necessary was the last thing he wanted. He hurried to the sickroom himself to see about the probability of a speedy departure. The doctor appeared ready to take his leave, smoothing his coat and giving his patient an encouraging pat on the shoulder. "Take heart that it's only a simple fracture," he said in a comforting tone. "You'll be up and around again in just a few weeks."

"Weeks?" The word slipped out before Willie could stop himself. He saw his own horror reflected in the lawyer's eyes.

"Are you telling me I'll be confined to this bed, helpless, for all that time?" Monroe demanded in a shaky voice.

"Probably not," the doctor replied with a jovial air that struck Willie as all too unconcerned. "If you mend well, you'll likely be up in a chair in ten days or so. You may even be able to walk with the aid of a crutch in a couple of weeks." He snapped the clasp shut on his medical bag and wagged a playful finger at Monroe. "Just remember where you set your things from now on so you don't fall over that valise again."

After the doctor had gone, Willie leaned against the door-jamb and eyed Monroe thoughtfully. "My mother says you've been mentioning the children. Would you like them to come pay their regards?"

Monroe's pale face took on an even more ashen hue. "No!" he yelped. "That is. . .not right away. I have been their protector for so long on this trip, it might cause them undue distress to see me in this weakened condition." He gave Willie a wan smile. "Perhaps in another day. Or maybe two."

Willie nodded and took refuge in the barn to work out his thoughts. He had no way to prove it, but if he didn't miss his guess, those kids had been involved in Monroe's so-called accident. . .right up to their angelic little necks.

He kicked at a dried corncob, sending it spinning across the barn floor in a crazy arc. There had to be some way to get that bunch back on the road again, and soon. Maybe they could ride on the train by themselves.

Willie brightened at the thought. Surely after one glimpse of those sweet little faces, some motherly soul could be prevailed upon to make sure they got as far as the stop where they'd take the stagecoach into Prescott. After that, it would be a matter of making sure they'd been safely stowed on the stage and were met by their guardian. A well-worded telegram or two should do the trick. It would be simple. He walked back to the house, growing more pleased with his plan by the minute.

He entered the door and stepped into a flurry of activity. "There you are. Thank goodness! I've been looking everywhere." His mother grabbed his shirtsleeve and pulled him along the corridor in her wake.

"What's wrong now? Did they— That is, Cousin Lewis hasn't taken a turn for the worse, has he?"

Without answering, his mother towed him to the invalid's room with the air of a conjurer producing a rabbit from a hat. "Here he is," she announced.

"Good," Charles said in a crisp tone. "There's just time

enough to make it."

"Make what?" Willie looked from one parent to the other, trying to make some sense of the conversation.

"Lewis feels it's important for the children to continue their journey immediately," his father told him.

"He's right," Willie said with conviction.

His mother beamed. "That's wonderful, Dear. I'm so glad you agree." She lowered her voice to a conspiratorial whisper. "Actually, the idea of them staying here any longer distresses him so much, your father and I are afraid it will affect his recovery. Poor Cousin Lewis! He takes his responsibilities so seriously."

Willie forbore to mention his suspicions of Cousin Lewis's real motive for wanting the children on their way. The reason didn't matter so long as those little troublemakers got on the train and left.

"Good, then it's settled." His father rose with the air of one satisfied with his accomplishment. "I knew we could count on you. The wagon's loaded and they're waiting on you."

"I'm on my way," Willie exulted. "Believe me, I wouldn't want to miss the chance to say good-bye."

His parents exchanged startled glances. "Didn't you tell him?" Charles demanded.

"There wasn't time," Abby explained. "I brought him straight here as soon as I found him." She laid her hand on Willie's arm. "You're not saying good-bye to them just yet. You're going to take them there. I've already packed a bag for you."

"To the train? I thought Hank—" He stopped himself in midsentence. It didn't matter; he could put up with them a bit longer. Nothing mattered, so long as they got out of his hair today.

"Not *to* the train, Dear. *On* the train."

A sick feeling of dread began in Willie's stomach and spread its tentacles through his chest and into every limb. "On?" His voice came out in a hoarse croak.

"That's right." His father clapped him on the shoulder. "We

needed someone to get those little tykes to Arizona, and you're just the man for the job. Now, hurry, or you'll miss your train."

Propelled between his parents, Willie exited the room. He turned for one last look at his traitorous cousin and met Monroe's gaze. In it, he felt sure he saw an expression of relief. . .mingled with a look of pity.

&

"Jessica, sit down. Toby, you too." Willie picked up the little boy and plopped him into the seat next to his sister, wincing when Toby's flailing boot connected with his shin.

"We've been on this train forever!" Jessica wailed.

"It hasn't been forever," Willie grumbled. It only seemed like it. Before this trip, he'd never have believed that three little kids could make a mere two days feel like an eternity. His eyelids drooped and his head began to nod. He caught himself up with a jolt. Every time he'd allowed himself to drowse, the kids had come up with yet another scheme to torment some unsuspecting passenger and make Willie look like the villain.

After a long night of horrified looks and scathing reprimands from the ladies on the train, Willie decided his only hope lay in staying awake until they'd reached the relative safety of the stagecoach. Surely even these three couldn't do too much within its confines. For now, though, he had to remain alert to prevent whatever devilment they might think of next.

He rolled his head from side to side and stifled a yawn. It would only take them another four hours to reach the junction at Ash Fork. He could hold out that long.

He angled himself so he could keep a watchful eye on the lot of them and fixed them with a stern glare. They stared back, all three chins jutted out in identical mutinous expressions. At least they'd dropped any pretense at being angelic so far as Willie was concerned. To the rest of the world, though, they kept up their cherubic facade while continuing to carry out their schemes and lay the blame at Willie's feet.

He shuddered. He didn't think he'd ever forget the expression on that elderly woman's face just before she went after him with her umbrella.

He only hoped their guardian had an iron constitution and nerves of steel. He'd need them.

&

"Next stop, Flagstaff." The conductor's voiced boomed through the car. "We'll only be here twenty minutes, folks. If you leave the train, don't go far."

Willie stretched and rubbed eyes that felt like they'd been filled with sand. His stomach rumbled. What could they find to eat in twenty minutes? He had to have something to keep up his strength. A hot meal might even make the kids mellow a bit. He got to his feet, ready to leave as soon as the car stopped.

The train lurched to a halt, and Willie shepherded his charges into a line in front of him. "Remember, I want you on your best behavior. Don't do anything that'll get us in trouble. Understand?"

Jessica sniffed and folded her arms. The boys merely scuffed their feet. Willie leaned forward and took the boys by the shoulders to make sure they'd paid attention to him, then felt his head jerked backward, his ear caught in a pincerlike grip. He turned to meet the baleful gaze of the heavyset woman who'd ridden across the aisle from them since Holbrook.

"Lay one hand on those precious babes, and I'll have the law after you," she threatened. "I've been watching you. You've badgered and hounded them ever since I got on this train. You're nothing but a bully."

Willie rubbed his ear and bit back a retort. Maybe he should have let Toby drop that bug into her open mouth while she was sleeping, after all. No, she'd only have found some reason to blame him for it. They all had.

He grabbed the younger children by the hand and led them across the dirt road to a clapboard building with the word Café lettered on its front. Three small tables filled the tiny space in front of the counter. Willie cast a quick glance at the chalkboard on the wall where the day's offerings were listed. "Could we get four bowls of venison stew as quickly as possible?"

The dour woman in charge nodded and set the bowls in front of them a few moments later. Willie relished each bite of the savory mixture, then set his spoon down with a sharp click. Wonderful! He felt better already. "Ready to go?" he asked the kids.

To his amazement, they'd barely touched their meals. "It's too hot," Toby complained.

"Well, hurry. We don't have too much time." He prodded at them, alternately pleading and threatening, until their bowls were empty. A warning whistle blast pierced the air. Good, they'd finished just in time.

"All right, back to the train," he commanded. To his relief, the Wingate trio filed out the door without protest. Outside, a spectacular sunset splayed streaks of crimson, pink, and gold across the sky. All four of them halted to take in the sight.

Willie closed his eyes in thanks for this reminder of the Lord's presence. If he focused on that truth instead of worrying what mischief the children might be plotting, he'd be able to manage the rest of the trip without losing his sanity. He stretched and breathed in a lungful of clear mountain air. With that dinner inside them, the kids just might fall asleep and give him the opportunity for a nap.

A bell began to ring, preparatory to the train leaving. "We'd better get going." He opened his eyes and froze. "Where's Toby?"

Frederick blinked up at him. "He said he needed to use the outhouse. Didn't you hear?"

"There's no time for that now! Where did he go?"

"Back there somewhere." Jessica pointed behind the café. "Do you want us to go ahead and get on the train?"

Willie darted a frantic glance from the children to the train, then to the shadows behind the building. He could hear the engine building up steam. "No, stay with me." He plunged into the alleyway, calling Toby's name.

"Over there!" Frederick cried.

Willie sprinted to the small wooden structure and pounded on the door. "Toby? Are you in there?"

"Yep."

"Get out here! We're going to miss the train." Another whistle punctuated his command.

"Can't."

Willie rattled the door against the latch. "What do you mean, you can't? The train's ready to leave." If he grabbed Toby under one arm and towed Jessica by the hand, maybe they could run fast enough to make it.

"Booaarrd!" The conductor's cry echoed along the alleyway.

"Toby, open this door!"

"Wait'll I get this button fastened."

"Now!" The locomotive's drive wheels squealed as they slipped, then caught on the steel rail.

"Almost got it. There!" Toby swung the outhouse door open, a triumphant smile on his face.

Willie scooped him up and grabbed Jessica's hand. "Hurry!" he shouted to Frederick. They raced onto the platform in time to see the last of the cars sweep past.

"Look!" Toby cried gleefully. "The man on the caboose is waving to me."

Jessica tugged at Willie's pant leg. "I'm tired," she whimpered.

"Me too," Frederick told him. "You'd probably better find us a room, since you didn't get us back here in time to catch the train."

Willie clenched his hands, bringing a yelp from Toby and a curious look from a passing lumberjack. With a supreme effort, he set the boy down and walked toward a board-and-batten building whose weathered front held a sign labeled Hotel.

❧

"Are we almost there yet?"

Willie stared at Frederick through bleary eyes and nodded. A day late, but almost there, ready to board the stagecoach for the last leg of this interminable journey.

He scrubbed his face with his hands, feeling the bristle of a day's worth of whiskers. It would be good to catch up with his luggage and his razor again. He probably looked downright scary, what with his haggard face and rumpled clothing. Sitting in a chair in front of their hotel room door last night hadn't given him the slightest bit of rest, but it had been the only way he felt sure he could keep the kids from doing another disappearing act.

"Next stop, Ash Fork." The train slowed and rumbled to a stop.

Willie pushed himself to his feet. "Come on," he said. "We have to pick up our luggage, then find the stage station."

"Will the stage leave right away, or will we stay in another hotel?" Toby asked. "I liked the hotel."

Willie stifled a growl and led his young charges to the station agent. "Where do we catch the stage?"

"Stage left this morning," the barrel-chested man told him, peering at Willie over his half-moon spectacles. "Won't be another one for three days. You the ones that missed the train yesterday? Your luggage is right over there."

Willie stared at the man, sure he'd heard wrong. "You mean there's no way to get to Prescott for three days?"

"Didn't say that," his informant replied. He paused to send a neat arc of tobacco juice into a nearby spittoon. "There's more than one way to get on down the road. You can ride, or you can rent a wagon over at the livery. You can even walk if you don't mind sand in your boots. Your choice." He walked away to inspect the freight that had just been delivered.

"Where's the stable?" Willie called to his retreating form.

"Right there." The man pointed with a stubby pencil, indicating a point halfway down the dusty street. " 'Cept the owner had to go out and check on his ranch. Won't be back 'til morning."

Willie bowed to the inevitable. "Grab those bags, Frederick," he said, picking up the largest two himself. "Looks like we'll be spending the night here."

Toby beamed. "Goody, another hotel!"

❧

Willie directed a sullen stare at the slowly unfolding land-scape and shifted on the wagon seat. Bundled in warm blankets purchased from the dry goods store, the three children dozed in the cool morning air, undisturbed by the wagon's constant jolting. Fine for them, getting to sleep all night and nap again during the day. He hadn't had a decent night's rest since they left the Double B.

Even the chair in the Flagstaff hotel room sounded good right about now, especially since their Ash Fork lodgings hadn't even boasted a chair and he'd wound up spending the night stretched out on the floor in front of the doorway. And that had been two nights ago. Last night's bed had been a blanket on the dirt at the side of the trail.

His head sagged, and he fought to hold it up again. If he figured right, they should get into Prescott by the following evening. . .if the wagon didn't lose a wheel, if they didn't encounter another canyon like the one they'd gone through yesterday, or if the rented horse didn't up and die on him.

Another day and a half. Then he'd hand the kids over to their guardian and head for the nearest hotel room. One he didn't have to share. One he could actually sleep in. A wistful smile curved his lips. He might not wake up for days.

"Williiee!" Jessica's shrill wail brought him out of his reverie. "I need to stop."

Muttering, he pulled the horse to a halt. When he'd figured the time the trip should take by wagon, he hadn't counted on all the stops a young child would need to make. Times three. Maybe they'd make it by summer.

❧

The next evening, Willie stopped the wagon at the top of a low rise and watched the gathering colors of his fifth Arizona sunset. By his calculations, Prescott should only be about five miles down the road. If he kept on, they could make it into town in another couple of hours or so. Not too late to locate

Thurman Hadlock, their guardian, and effect the transfer of the Wingates and their belongings. Not too late to find the bed that beckoned so tantalizingly in his imagination.

On the other hand. . . He glanced over his shoulder at the grubby children slumped in the wagon bed. The long, bumpy drive had taken the starch out of both them and their clothing. At the moment, they looked more like street urchins than heirs of a fair-sized inheritance. This job hadn't been his idea, but he wouldn't want to give Hadlock the impression he'd slacked off on his responsibilities. And he might as well give the poor man hope, at least in the beginning.

An hour later, the kids had been scrubbed until their faces glowed a rosy hue. The boys had their hair combed, and Jessica's hung in a neat braid. Their good clothes lay spread across the wagon bed, ready to don first thing in the morning. With sweet smiles, the three siblings snuggled down into their blankets on the far side of the fire.

Willie stared at their slumbering forms in wonder. They really did look angelic when they were asleep. Too bad he couldn't deliver them to their guardian before they woke up.

He took a few weary steps toward the water bucket, then looked at his bedroll and hesitated. With all three children safely asleep, he couldn't pass up this opportunity to catch up on some much needed rest. He could just as well clean up and shave in the morning.

He pulled off his boots and stretched out on his blanket with a blissful sigh. He wouldn't do more than doze. Just the chance to close his eyes without worrying what the kids might be getting into would be heavenly. He settled his head on his rolled-up coat and pulled the blanket around his shoulders to ward off the chill evening air. Just a few minutes' sleep; that's all he needed.

four

Fingers of light probed at Willie's eyelids. He cracked one eye open, blinked, then came fully awake when he realized the sun had already topped the mountains. He leaped to his feet. He couldn't remember the last time he'd slept this late. That's what came of trying to stay awake for days on end. At least now he'd be rested and ready to face the day and the kids.

They must have slept late, too. He hadn't heard a peep out of them. Maybe he'd wait to wake them until he spruced up. Then they'd head into town, find Thurman Hadlock, and say their farewells. Grinning at the thought of imminent freedom, he got up to draw some water from the barrel and froze.

The wagon was gone.

So were the kids.

On closer inspection, so were his boots.

Willie raked his fingers through his hair and stared wildly, unable to take in the meaning of the empty campsite. He circled their camp area in his stocking feet, looking for something that would tell him what had happened. This didn't make a bit of sense. Maybe he was still asleep.

"Ouch!" A pinecone jabbed his foot, assuring him he was awake. Choosing his steps with care, he went to the spot where he'd parked the wagon the night before. The tracks told the story. Three small sets of footprints led to the rear of the wagon and dug more deeply into the dirt where they'd pushed it thirty yards away from camp. At the bottom of the gentle incline, the largest set of prints left the wagon, then returned, accompanied by the hoofprints of the missing horse.

It didn't take much of a tracker to figure out the rest of the tale. The little miscreants had harnessed the horse and started it out at a slow walk until safely out of earshot. Then they'd picked up the pace and gone on their merry way, following the road to town. Willie shaded his eyes against the sun and scanned the terrain ahead but couldn't spot them even as a speck in the distance.

"Of all the lowdown, rotten tricks!" Willie kicked at the ground in disgust and yelped when he stubbed his toe on a rock. Wait until he got his hands on those little thieves. He pulled on his coat, threw his blanket over his shoulder, and hobbled off down the road muttering dire threats between clenched teeth.

A mile down the road, he peeled off his socks. With the soles worn away to mere shreds, they did no more than irritate his feet. A mile farther, he spotted something dangling from an oak branch and whooped when he recognized his boots. After checking inside them first, he pulled them on and immediately wished he'd kept his socks. The leather rubbed the raw spots on his tender feet. He could envision the crop of blisters he'd get from this.

Dust rose up in little clouds with every step he took. The chill of the spring morning had long since worn off. He tossed the blanket under a scrubby bush, then pulled off his coat and slung it over his shoulder. When he topped a low hill, he paused, frowning.

The road forked here. The well-traveled road to town ran straight ahead, winding down the other side of the hill to disappear in the distance, while the smaller fork curved off. The wagon tracks followed the curve.

What could those kids be up to? The thought of them wandering off course so close to their destination made him quicken his painful strides. It wouldn't do to let them get lost, tempting though it might be.

Up ahead the tracks turned to the left, and Willie pulled up short when he spotted the empty wagon sitting in front of a neatly kept farmhouse. All the frustration and humiliation of the past week rose up to blur his thinking. With visions of mayhem dancing in his head, he crossed the open farmyard, stomped up the porch steps, and pounded on the front door.

A moment later, the door swung open to reveal a slender young woman with glossy dark hair and startling blue eyes that focused on him with ill-concealed dislike.

"Yes?" she said in a glacial tone.

Willie was in no mood for polite conversation. "The three kids who came in that wagon—are they here?"

The woman regarded him coolly. "They are." She made no move to call them but gripped the door with one hand and planted the other firmly on the doorjamb.

"Well, send them out!" Willie barked.

"Absolutely not." She lifted her chin and stared at him defiantly.

Willie gaped. "Why not? I'm supposed to have them." When she only glared at him in silence, he tried again. "They are my responsibility," he told her, enunciating each word with care. She didn't seem simpleminded, but appearances could be deceiving. "You don't need to be bothered with them anymore."

"Bothered?" Angry sparks flashed in those amazing blue eyes. "Is that all those children are to you, a bother? No wonder they don't want to be anywhere near you."

"Don't want to—"

"They came here early this morning and asked for sanctuary." A crystal droplet formed in one corner of her eye at the recollection. "I didn't understand it at first, but after meeting you, I can fully comprehend why." She drew herself up to her full height, which put the top of her head in the vicinity of Willie's shoulder.

"I don't want to keep them," he spluttered. "Not permanently, anyway. I'm bringing them out here to deliver them to their guardian. As soon as I turn them over to him, they'll never have to look at me again."

He made a quick mental calculation. If they left in the next few minutes, they could probably reach Prescott in a little over an hour. Allow another hour or so to locate Hadlock and effect the transfer of responsibility. By early afternoon, he ought to be soaking in the hottest bathwater he could persuade the local hotel keeper to provide. If this misguided female would quit interfering with his plans.

Her look thawed a few degrees. "Their guardian? Then the poor little dears are orphans? Oh, how sad."

Willie bit his tongue and refrained from telling her to save her sympathy for Hadlock, the citizens of Prescott, and quite possibly the whole of Arizona Territory.

She appeared to waver. "I suppose that does put it in a different light, Mister. . ."

"Bradley. Willie Bradley," he said heartily. "Sure it does. So if you'll just call them now, we'll be on our way. You wouldn't be able to tell me where to find Mr. Hadlock, I suppose?"

"Hadlock? Thurman Hadlock?"

"That's right. Do you know him?"

Her softening expression congealed into one of horrified distaste. "Thurman Hadlock isn't fit to raise a dog, much less these precious little ones. You might as well be on your way, Mr. Bradley. I will not be a party to sending innocent children into the care of the likes of that man. They were right; they do need protection." She slammed the door, missing Willie's nose by a mere inch.

"Hey!" He raised his hand to knock again but heard the *thunk* of the bar dropping firmly into place. He stared at the solid panel, nonplussed, then moved to one side to see if he could glimpse anything through a crack in the curtains covering the front window.

An alarming sight met his eyes: a wild-eyed, unshaven creature with tufts of hair standing on end like a porcupine's quills. Willie grimaced at the sight of his image reflected in the glass. No wonder she hadn't trusted him. He wouldn't trust anyone who looked like that, either.

Now what? He stepped down off the porch and kicked at a rock. He had to get those kids back, but how could he convince—why hadn't he asked her name?—how could he convince that human watchdog to talk to him again? The sooner he shed those kids, the sooner he could get back to the Double B. He aimed another kick at the hapless stone. An idea took shape in his mind. He found the rented horse in the barn, hitched it to the wagon, and set off toward Prescott.

&

"Is he gone?"

Violet Canfield knelt before the wide-eyed youngsters clustered in the hallway and touched the little girl's flaxen hair in a comforting manner. "He's gone, Jessie. You don't need to worry anymore."

"Thank you, Miss Violet," the older boy said solemnly. "You saved us."

Violet blinked back tears at their gratitude and obvious relief. She couldn't blame them a bit for being glad to see that odious man leave. How frightened the poor dears must have been! Why, his unkempt appearance had been enough to unnerve the stoutest heart, much less these tender children.

"Can we stay with you?" the littlest one asked, speaking around the finger stuck in his mouth.

"Of course you can," she reassured him.

"Cross your heart?"

"Absolutely. Let's find places for all of you to sleep." She led the way to the cupboard, where she pulled out fresh linens, then set about assigning the children to their places.

"Frederick, you and Toby will stay in here." She pushed aside the brief flicker of uneasiness at the thought of Rachel and Daniel's probable reaction to learning their bedroom had been taken over by a pair of young boys. They wouldn't be back for weeks yet. By then, the question of the children's permanent residence would have been settled. She stripped the sheets off the bed, replaced them with the clean bedding, and pulled the comforter neatly into place.

Leaving the boys to settle their belongings in their temporary home, she led Jessica along the short hallway. "And how would you like to stay in this room? It belonged to my father."

She swept open the curtains to let light flood the room and turned to see the little girl's reaction.

Jessie gazed at the cozy bed and offered her a shy smile. "I like it," she said. "It's much nicer than sleeping on the ground."

"I don't doubt it." Violet pressed her lips together in a prim line while she set about making the bed. *The man must be a monster,* she concluded, shaking the pillow into a clean, crisp case. *Forcing these tiny things to sleep out in the open. The very idea!* She thumped the pillow into place.

Rachel often accused her of being flighty and dreamy, but there had been nothing dreamy about the way she'd sent Mr. Willie Bradley packing, she remembered with satisfaction. Recalling the look on his face when she swung the door closed, she almost wished Rachel had been there to see her in action.

Almost.

"Don't bring home any strays." Her sister's teasing admonition echoed in her ears. But surely Rachel had been referring to stray animals, not these adorable, homeless waifs.

And, she reminded herself virtuously, she hadn't brought them home; they had come to her of their own volition. The Lord must have directed them straight to her door for protection. Even Rachel wouldn't ask her to fly in the face of divine guidance. In a way, all the wounded creatures she'd cared for over the years—the countless injured birds, rabbits, and squirrels she'd taken in and tended—might have been practice for just this purpose.

The story of Queen Esther flashed into her mind. What was it Esther's uncle told her when she shrank from putting herself in danger in order to save her people? "Who knoweth whether thou art come to the kingdom for such a time as this?"

"That's it," Violet murmured. "God prepared me for such a time as this." She gave Jessica a quick squeeze and headed for the kitchen to decide what she'd fix for dinner. For herself, a slice of bread with honey would have sufficed, but her new houseguests needed a more nourishing meal. No telling what that contemptible man had forced them to eat while on the trail, if he'd fed them at all.

Violet lifted her book from the dining table and closed it with a tender smile. She'd been looking forward to continuing her perusal of knightly adventures and daring rescues while she ate her lunch, but it could wait. Now she was in the midst of her own adventure. A shiver of delight ran up her arms.

She hummed while she prepared a hearty soup. She hated to admit it, but even her storybook heroes with their tales of derring-do hadn't kept her from being a trifle lonely these past few days. Not that she'd grown tired of them. Who could grow weary of reading the exploits of Robin Hood and Sir Galahad again and again? But it did make a wonderful change to be needed by living, breathing people.

She stirred the bubbling soup, savoring its rich aroma. Rachel and Daniel both teased her mercilessly about her penchant for tales of high adventure and romance, urging her to get her head out of the clouds and look at the young men available in the area instead of waiting for a white knight to appear and sweep her off her feet.

Violet had always ignored them, determined to hold out for the man of her dreams. She knew as surely as she breathed that one day he would come into her life and nothing would ever be the same again.

"And just where do you think this hero of yours will come from?" Rachel would scoff. "Do you expect him to appear out of nowhere?"

It would happen. It couldn't be as impossible as her sister made it sound. After all, she reasoned, that disreputable Bradley person had dropped into her life right out of the blue only that morning. But he hardly fit the picture of a hero.

The sound of children's voices drifted in through the window. Violet smiled. Good, they'd found something to play with outside. How nice that they felt so much at home already! She pulled out a bowl and began to mix up a batch of biscuits. A flash of gray caught her attention and she glanced outside. One of the farm cats ran streaking off toward the barn, emitting a plaintive yowl.

Odd, she thought. The cats didn't usually run from people. But then, they weren't used to children.

five

Time spent with soap and water made a man feel almost as good as a good night's sleep, Willie decided. Having the water barrel, his luggage, and a bit of privacy again, he'd taken the opportunity to clean up and shave. He squared his shoulders, feeling more like himself than he had in days.

He hoped his efforts improved his appearance as much as his morale; he didn't want anyone else looking at him the way that stubborn young woman had. His high spirits dropped a notch, remembering her disdainful expression. He might not have the authority his father did, but he had grown used to people treating him with a certain amount of respect as the son of the Double B's owner. Being viewed as though he were some loathsome insect was a new experience for him, and an unwelcome one.

After making arrangements for the horse and wagon to be returned to Ash Fork and renting a light gray gelding for use during his brief stay, he asked for directions and soon found himself seated in a straight-backed chair explaining his predicament to Sheriff John Dolan.

The lanky, slow-talking lawman leaned back in his chair and pursed his lips. "Sounds like you have yourself a problem, all right. Now, who did you say you left the kids with?"

Willie gulped. "We didn't exactly get as far as introductions," he admitted.

The flicker of a smile lifted one corner of Dolan's mouth. "All right. Can you describe the place and the woman?" He listened to Willie's account and nodded. "That'd be Violet Canfield, from the sound of it."

He squinted his eyes into thoughtful slits and gave Willie a measuring look. "She does tend to be a mite dreamy, but all in all she's got a good head on her shoulders. I can't see why she'd hesitate to do the right thing." He leaned forward and drummed his fingers on the desktop. "You didn't do anything to make her suspicious, did you? Or uncomfortable?" He eyed Willie with a narrow gaze that sent chills of apprehension racing up and down his spine.

"No!" Willie's conscience prodded him. "Well, maybe I did look a little wild, not having washed up and shaved and all. That might not have set well with her."

"Uh-huh."

"And I might have raised my voice a bit a time or two," he mumbled.

"Mm."

Willie felt a flush rise up his neck and heat his face. "You don't know what those kids are like," he protested. "They'd try the patience of a saint. All right, I admit she probably thought I was some kind of thug. The bottom line is, those kids are my responsibility until I can turn them over to Thurman Hadlock. And speaking of Hadlock, I don't suppose you could tell me where to find him? We could get this whole thing straightened out in a matter of minutes."

Dolan, who'd seemed to accept his report readily enough up to this point, gauged him again with a gaze that made Willie want to squirm in his chair. "Hadlock, eh? You know the man?"

"I've never met him. All I know is what I was told by my mother's cousin, the lawyer I told you about. Hadlock was a close friend of the kids' father and was designated as their legal guardian in the event of his death." He produced a letter of introduction and handed it over to Dolan, who perused it briefly.

"Looks sound enough." Dolan slid the letter across the desk and tipped his chair back on two legs.

Willie breathed freely again. This would not be a man he'd choose to cross if he could help it.

Dolan rocked forward, appearing to have reached a decision. He planted his hands on his desk and pushed himself upright. "I can tell you where Hadlock lives and where he usually spends his time. Don't know that it'll do you a lot of good, though. I can't recall seeing him recently. In the meantime," he said, settling his hat on his head, "let's head out to the farm and see if we can't get your situation with Miss Canfield squared away."

Willie's misgivings returned during their ride out. "I hope the place is still standing," he told Dolan, and detailed his experiences with the young Wingates. "I've never seen anything like them."

Dolan shook his head dismissively. "Sounds to me like all they need is a firm hand and someone who won't put up with nonsense."

Willie started to argue, then broke off. "You may be right," he said, eyeing the sheriff appraisingly. "I don't suppose you'd be interested in taking care of them until I can turn them over to Hadlock? You sound like just the man for the job."

"Nope." Dolan dashed Willie's rising hopes with the single word. "My job's to maintain law and order, not nursemaid a passel of young'uns." He turned his horse into the path to Violet's home. With a sigh of resignation, Willie followed.

❧

Violet sloshed her hands through the soapy water, checking for any errant dishes that might have escaped her notice. Lunch had gone well, she thought smugly. The children's table manners showed they'd received proper training. Now Toby lay stretched out on Rachel and Daniel's bed, and Jessie and Frederick played a quiet game of checkers in the living room. Violet grinned. What was so hard about taking care of children?

She wiped the last plate and set it in the cupboard, then glanced out the kitchen window. Two riders approached the hitching rail out front. *If this isn't the day for unexpected arrivals!* Violet dried her hands and hung her apron on its hook. Smoothing her skirt, she hurried to the front door and peeped out the adjacent window.

She smiled when she recognized John Dolan's tall bay. His easygoing personality and dry humor always made him a welcome guest. But who could the other man be? The slim rider dismounted in one fluid movement. The gray horse he rode gleamed in the afternoon sunlight. *Is it my white knight at last?* Violet chuckled at her flight of fancy.

Waiting until the men's boots rang on the wooden porch, she swung the door open wide with a smile of welcome. "Sheriff! It's good to see you."

She peered past him to see if she could identify his companion. The tall man's chestnut hair fell across his forehead above lively blue eyes. Eyes that reminded her of. . .who? With a start, Violet recognized her unwelcome visitor of that morning. Her eyes narrowed to slits.

"Afternoon, Violet," Dolan said. "I see you remember Mr. Bradley here."

Violet crossed her arms and blocked the doorway. "Unfortunately." She felt gratified when Dolan's companion looked away.

The sheriff leaned back on the porch rail. "What's this I hear about you sending him away with a flea in his ear and not letting him have those kids that came out with him?"

She lifted her chin. "It's true, Sheriff. You see, when I went out to sweep the porch this morning, I saw three children turning their wagon into the drive. They were obviously frightened and told me all about Mr. Bradley and his treatment of them."

Distracted only momentarily by Bradley's sputter of protest, she refocused her attention on the lawman and went on. "They asked for shelter; I gave it to them. It's as simple as that. When he turned up several hours later, his behavior only confirmed everything they had told me. I refused to allow him near them," she said, "and what's more, I still do."

Dolan lifted his hand in a placating gesture. "Now, Violet—"

"Mr. Bradley has obviously managed to worm his way into your good graces. You wouldn't have been so quick to approve of him if you'd seen him in his previous state."

Bradley fixed her with a hostile stare and opened his mouth for the first time since his arrival. "I wouldn't have looked like that if those kids hadn't made off with the wagon and the water and my clean clothes." His voice rose louder with every word.

Violet looked at the sheriff triumphantly. "See what I mean?"

"Hmm." Dolan stroked his chin. "He has some papers with him, though, drawn up all legal and proper. He's supposed to be taking these young'uns to their guardian."

"Thurman Hadlock!" Violet summed up her opinion of the man in one contemptuous sniff.

Dolan drew himself up into a more official-looking stance. "Be that as it may, the law's the law, and I have to see that it's carried out. This man not only has a legal right but a moral responsibility to turn those children over to the person their father chose to raise them, whether any of us would approve of that choice or not."

He turned to the man beside him, who stood grinning at Violet's discomfiture. "On the other hand," he drawled, "there's no telling where all you'll have to look to find Hadlock, and you probably won't want the kids underfoot the whole time."

Violet suppressed a laugh when the grin faded and a puzzled frown appeared below the lock of hair that insisted on falling over his forehead.

"I'm suggesting a compromise," Dolan continued. "Why not let the kids stay here under Violet's care while you do your searching? That way you'll both be happier, and those youngsters won't have to be dragged around from pillar to post. Sounds to me like they've been through enough already." He rocked back on his heels and looked from one to the other. "What do you think?"

Violet gave him her brightest smile. "It suits me fine, Sheriff."

Obvious relief broke across Bradley's face. "Sounds good to me, too. That's probably the best thing for everyone all around, especially if it takes a day or so to find this fellow."

"Then it's settled." Dolan nodded to Violet with a pleased smile. "You'll know they're being well cared for, and you'll have your sister to help in case things get out of hand."

Violet cleared her throat. "Well. . ."

The sheriff gave her a questioning look.

She drew herself erect. "Actually, Rachel and Daniel are in Tucson right now." She bristled at Dolan's skeptical frown. Why did everyone always assume she couldn't handle the smallest job without help? "But I'm sure I'll do fine without them."

"You mean you're here all by yourself?" Bradley's tone went from agreeable to worried. "Just you and the kids? Alone?"

Violet stiffened. "I assure you, I am more than capable of caring for three small children."

"Lady, you have no idea what you're taking on. Just be grateful those three haven't burned your house down. . .yet."

Dolan inserted himself between them and laid his hand on the other man's shoulder. "Son, you'd best never question a woman's ability. I'm sure Miss Violet will do a fine job." He glanced at Violet, concern shadowing his face. "Won't you?"

"Of course I will," she snapped. "How much trouble can three youngsters be?"

❧

It took all Willie's self-control to keep from chortling aloud at that last remark. It showed just how little Miss Violet Canfield knew about children. He smirked, remembering that defiant tilt to her chin when she'd declared herself equal to the task of taking care of the Wingates. The Wingates! He nearly hooted out loud. She had no idea what she'd gotten herself into, no idea at all. . .but she'd find out soon enough. He'd be willing to bank on it.

In all honesty, Willie had to admit she probably could handle any normal child who crossed her path. When her eyes weren't shooting out angry blue sparks or gazing at him with cold suspicion, they held a gentle, friendly light. More than likely, she got along with most kids just fine. Children in general weren't all that bad. Even his four young cousins, rowdy as they could be at times, could be brought under control with just a bit of effort.

But Miss Canfield wasn't dealing with normal children. She'd elected to take on a handful of Wingates. And regardless of her good intentions, until the legalities had been observed, the final responsibility for them and their conduct lay at Willie's feet.

He supposed he ought to show some concern for their well-being. "Are they really all right? Well fed and all that?"

Violet fixed him with an austere gaze. "I can assure you they've settled in and are quite comfortable."

As if to corroborate her statement, a sleepy-eyed Toby appeared in the doorway. When he saw Willie, he clung to Violet's skirt. She smoothed his hair with a gentle hand and smiled down at him. The little boy looked up at her with what Willie could only describe as a nauseating simper. Violet turned a triumphant glance upon Willie. Immediately, the little boy stuck out his tongue. Willie took a half step toward him, and at once Toby began to whimper.

"There, there," Violet soothed him. "You're going to stay right here with me, Sweetheart." The little boy looked up at her with a questioning gaze. Violet gave the tip of his nose a playful tap with her finger. "Cross my heart," she whispered.

Sweetheart? The endearment made Willie want to gag, but he forced himself to step back and assume what he hoped looked like a nonthreatening expression. He shot a glance toward Dolan, wondering if the sharp-eyed sheriff had caught the little byplay. He'd be willing to bet the man didn't miss much. Dolan, however, maintained an impassive mien. Willie sighed. It would boost his spirits to know that someone besides himself recognized the Wingates' subterfuge.

Instead, the sheriff straightened and settled his Stetson on his head. "Seeing as how you folks are all set, it looks like it's time for me to be moving on."

"Then I'll say good-bye to you both," Violet said. "Where may I contact you if I need you, Mr. Bradley?"

Willie's jaw sagged. Up until that moment, he hadn't considered what his lodging arrangements might be. He'd noticed a hotel in town, but since he hadn't completed his mission by handing over the kids, he hadn't gotten around to inquiring about a room. Surely they wouldn't be booked up, though. He opened his mouth to say he could be found there, but his conscience stopped him.

Much as he'd love being away from the Wingates, they were still his responsibility. He couldn't foist them off on a total stranger. Besides, the idea of stranding her alone with that threesome, no matter how angelic she believed them to be, made his blood run cold. No telling what they might get up to if they didn't have a restraining influence close at hand.

"I'm still accountable for them." He chose his words with care. "It wouldn't do for me to just take off and leave them."

Violet pressed one hand to her throat and her brow crinkled. "I hadn't thought about that. I'll admit you have a right to want to be close by, but. . ." Her voice trailed away, then her face brightened.

"I think I have a solution," she said with a radiant smile that made Willie blink. "There's a small cabin on the far side of the barn that might suit your purpose nicely. My brother-in-law, Daniel, put it up some time ago. You're welcome to use it if you like. It might take a bit of fixing up and cleaning," she added sweetly, "but I'm sure you won't mind. . .and I certainly won't have time to do it with three children to cook and care for."

She flashed another dazzling smile at the men. "Good-bye, Sheriff. Thank you for taking care of this little difficulty so easily. Come, Toby. We need to see what your brother and sister are doing." With that, she shepherded the little boy back inside the house and closed the door. Softly, this time.

Willie beamed at the sheriff. "Looks like things are going to work out just fine. I'll spend a few minutes straightening up my new digs and start looking for Hadlock this evening."

"Mm." Dolan rubbed his hand across his chin. "That place out back of the barn, huh? Last time I saw it. . .well, you may not want to plan on going much of anywhere today." With that cryptic remark, he untied his horse from the hitching rail and swung into his saddle. "If I remember right," he called over his shoulder, "Daniel keeps his tools just inside the barn door."

Willie stared after Dolan's departing figure, then scratched his head and circled around the barn. Maybe the sheriff assumed he wouldn't be used to roughing it a bit. But why? He didn't look like some slicked-up city dude, did he? The cabin might not be anything special, but he could surely put up with a little privation for a night or two.

He rounded the barn and stopped dead in his tracks. A cabin, did she say? More like a pile of rubble. He walked around the tumbledown shack, moving carefully so as not to knock it over. As far as he could tell, it had only been a ramshackle, thrown-together affair to begin with. With the passage of time, the walls leaned inward in an attempt to meet one another, and the roof had begun to droop below wall level.

A little fixing up, huh? Willie snorted. He had a notion to go back and tell Violet just what he thought of her little cabin, but he had a feeling she'd enjoy it too much. He headed toward the barn to search for a hammer and nails.

When the sun hovered at the edge of the horizon, Willie stood back and appraised his progress. The four walls stood more or less erect, and the roof no longer threatened imminent collapse. Underneath the rubble he had found what could pass for a cot, once he beat the dust out of the thin mattress. Not much, but then, he didn't need much more than a roof over his head for the next night or two.

At least the place had a door. After a moment's reflection, he scrounged through the pile of scrap lumber and fashioned a sturdy latch. He didn't intend to stay awake all through his limited stay, and he had no desire for the Wingates to catch him napping. Memories of Lewis Monroe's "accident" remained all too fresh in his mind.

After a final scrutiny, he walked up to the house and rapped on the kitchen door. Violet answered his knock and clapped one hand to her mouth. Her eyes flared wide. "Oh, dear," she said in a choked voice.

Willie rolled his eyes. He hoped she didn't plan to do a repeat performance of their first meeting every time he came to the house alone. "I'd like to borrow a broom," he said. "And a scrub brush and pail, if you don't mind."

Muffled giggles met his ears when she moved to fetch the cleaning supplies, and he saw the three children seated at the table, staring at him with undisguised glee. What was the matter with everyone around here?

Violet returned and handed him the requested items. "Here you are, Mr. Bradley. While you're scrubbing out the cabin, I'll try to find a spare pitcher and basin for you." She tilted her head and gave him an appraising glance. "You have a much less frightening appearance when you're clean, you know."

Willie looked down at his clothes. If the rest of him looked anything like his filthy shirt and pants, no wonder his arrival had created a sensation.

"We haven't used the place much since my sister and brother-in-law got married," Violet went on. Her lips twitched. "I guess we really haven't done much to keep it up, have we?" She reached out and brushed at his ear, then held out her hand. "Here. You might be able to find a better place for this." She draped a large cobweb across his outstretched palm. More giggles erupted from behind her.

Without a word, Willie picked up the things he had asked for and stomped back down the path to scrub his sorry cabin, knock the dust out of his sorry mattress, and settle down on his sorry cot for his first night in his temporary home.

six

The late afternoon sun's rays found their way under Willie's hat brim and hit him square in the eyes. He tipped the brim forward and lowered his chin. Settling back in the saddle, he let his horse have its head. After ten days of traveling back and forth between the Canfield farm and Prescott, he had no problem finding the way.

Another day of dead ends. Willie's stomach knotted. How hard should it be to locate one man in a close-knit frontier community? The territorial capital boasted two thousand souls, and not one of them claimed to know the whereabouts of Thurman Hadlock.

Most seemed to know about him, though. Willie winced, recalling the names he'd heard Hadlock called just that day: lush, gambler, and reprobate being the most repeatable terms. His shoulder still ached where a gray-haired woman swatted it repeatedly with her broom at the mere mention of Hadlock's name.

The most charitable opinion he'd heard came from a store-keeper who told him, "When Hadlock came here four years ago, he seemed respectable enough. Probably was. But being out on the frontier like this either makes or breaks a man. Hadlock's one who broke."

To top it all off, Willie's conscience started sending out annoying messages, asking whether it would really be right to place three children with a man who had popular opinion so firmly set against him. He still held the notion that the Wingate progeny were little fiends with angels' faces, but even so, he didn't know if he could leave them with someone like that with any sense of indifference.

He straightened in the saddle, as though by doing so he

could shake off his doubts. Their father knew the man well enough to trust him with the upbringing of his children, he reminded himself. And his mother's cousin Lewis, a bona fide lawyer, seemed comfortable enough in bringing them out here to him.

True, a niggling inner voice carped at him, *but Monroe hadn't gotten this far and seen what you have.*

On the other hand, Monroe was currently laid up in bed suffering from a mysteriously broken leg. He'd do well to remember that when his sympathies threatened to get the best of him.

The horse took the turn off the main road without any prodding, and Willie reviewed that day's progress. He had finally located Hadlock's place. The pitiful collection of rawhide and baling wire hadn't eased Willie's misgivings one whit. It might be several steps above the shack Willie resided in at the moment, but nowhere near the kind of home a fellow ought to have to raise a family.

He'd looked around but couldn't find any trace of the man. Worse, he hadn't been able to see any indication he'd been home at all in recent days. A check of the usual haunts Dolan mentioned turned up nothing but a sense of distaste both for the places Hadlock frequented and the company he kept. The horse flinched when a cottontail scampered across the trail, and Willie gave him a soothing pat on the neck.

When he left New Mexico, he never dreamed the job would take so long. There had to be some way to resolve his dilemma, but he didn't know what. He'd even gone to the extreme of sending Monroe a telegram, asking if he should take the kids back to the Double B until the lawyer had recovered sufficiently to return with them himself. It cost his ego plenty to hint he might not be able to handle this job, but he didn't know what else to do.

There had been one bright moment in his otherwise unprofitable day. He brightened at the memory. Coming out of Grady's Market, he'd walked straight into a passing young lady. The collision sent her parcels flying out of her arms and knocked her flat.

Mortified by his clumsiness, he rushed to help her up, then scrambled to retrieve the packages scattered across the boardwalk. Much to his relief, she accepted his fumbling apology with grace.

"Goodness me, I should have been watching where I was going," she said, peeping up at him past the flowered brim of her bonnet. Eyes the color of spring grass shone with good humor, and she favored him with a brilliant smile that caused a tiny dimple to appear on her ivory cheek.

Willie's jaw dropped so far he wouldn't have been surprised to hear it echo off the boardwalk. He made an effort to raise it back into place. He'd already acted like a blundering idiot in bowling her over; no point in making a complete fool of himself besides. "I'm. . .I'm so sorry."

She tilted her head back and gave a merry laugh. Under the bonnet's wide brim, strands of golden hair shimmered in the sunlight. "You're forgiven. Would you mind escorting me home? I got a bit carried away with my shopping, and I'm afraid these parcels are going to be too much for me."

Willie didn't wait for another chance to redeem himself. With a gallant sweep of his hat, he took her packages with one arm and offered her the other.

"I'm Mary Rose Downey, by the way," she said, her enchanting face turned up to his. "And you're. . .?"

Willie felt a flush creep up his neck. Couldn't he remember the simplest manners his mother had instilled over the years? "I'm Willie Bradley. And I'm pleased to meet you."

Mary Rose strolled down the street at an easy pace. "How long have you been in Prescott? You're either new here or you've been keeping to yourself. Otherwise I certainly would have noticed you."

The flush rose to his cheeks and forehead. Did she mean what he hoped she did? "I've been here just over a week. I'm staying out at the Canfield place."

Mary Rose raised a delicate eyebrow. "Are you a relative, or. . . ?" Her voice trailed away into silence.

"No, nothing like that," he hastened to explain. "I brought three orphaned kids out here to meet their guardian. A man named Thurman Hadlock." He waited for her reaction and felt relieved when she only nodded. "Miss Canfield's watching the kids for me while I look for him."

"Miss Canfield? Violet, you mean?" The unblemished brow puckered in a tiny frown. "But I thought I heard she'd gone to Tucson."

Willie chuckled. "No, her sister and her husband are the ones who are gone. Violet's still here."

Both eyebrows raised at that revelation.

Willie thought he'd burn up with embarrassment. What was it about this woman that made him unable to express the simplest thought clearly? "It's not what you're thinking," he sputtered. "Not at all. The children are staying in the house with her. I'm in a cabin out back." He watched her face intently and relaxed when her radiant smile returned.

"I see." She squeezed his arm in an intimate gesture that sent his pulse from a trot to a gallop. "I have a suggestion," she said, slowing her steps to stop in front of a handsome two-story house. "I know just about everybody in town. Why don't I help you look for Mr. Hadlock?"

"Why, sure. If you really want to." Had he really found someone willing to help instead of running him off at the mention of Hadlock's name?

"Wonderful." The dimple appeared once more. "Why don't you pick me up right here tomorrow morning? My father has a lot of business connections. He might be able to use his influence to help too."

"That would be great. I'm sure glad I bumped into you. I mean. . .I would appreciate that very much." He left with her musical laugh ringing in his ears.

Mary Rose's help might not locate Hadlock any sooner, he reflected while he turned his horse into Violet's drive, but it would sure make looking for him a lot more pleasant.

❧

"More potatoes?" Violet passed the earthenware bowl in response to Willie's nod and tried to maintain the bright smile she'd plastered on her face in preparation for the evening meal. Every weary bone in her body cried out for rest, but she had no intention of letting him know how exhausted she felt. Everyone seemed to think she had her head in the clouds too much to be able to do anything useful on her own. That assumption tired her as much as taking care of the children did.

She slid Toby's plate closer, the better to cut his chicken into smaller bites. How could three little children add so many extra duties to her day? When Daniel and Rachel first left for Tucson, time stretched before her like an unending ribbon of days, hers to fill in any way she chose. Today the happy hours she'd whiled away with her favorite books seemed a distant dream.

Instead, her days were filled with chores from sunup to sunset with no time to even think of having a few spare minutes to spend reading. Taking care of injured animals had involved little more than binding up their wounds, fashioning some sort of bed, and feeding them at intervals. Plenty of time remained for whatever chores awaited her, with hours left over to follow her own pursuits.

Now her waking hours revolved around cooking, cleaning, and doing laundry, plus gathering eggs and taking care of the livestock. Doing these household chores for herself hadn't presented a problem; the additional load of three people—four, counting Willie, since he ate with them and had taken her up on her offer to do his laundry—threatened to overwhelm her.

Not that she intended to admit that to a living soul! She took a bite of mashed potatoes and gravy, and her gaze fell on her most recent letter from Rachel, in its place on the sideboard. All was well, she wrote. She and Daniel were enjoying the warmer weather in the southern part of the territory. Daniel still had several mining properties to look over, which might take a couple of weeks longer than they'd thought. If Violet had no objection, they might delay their return for awhile.

Violet's guilty glance rested momentarily on the reply she'd penned that afternoon, waiting for Willie to take it to town with him tomorrow on his latest foray in search of Thurman Hadlock.

Had she done wrong by letting Rachel think nothing had changed since her departure? She'd filled her letter with cheery talk about the weather and signs of the approaching spring, news about the farm, and the latest news from town, all written in a bright, breezy tone. She hadn't lied— exactly—by failing to let her sister know their home had four new residents, but the omission gnawed at her.

It would only worry Rachel, she rationalized. *Time enough to let her know when she gets back. She's had little enough time alone with Daniel since they married; no point in making her feel she needs to rush home to be sure I'm not botching everything.*

Rachel and Daniel hadn't taken the time for a honeymoon when they married a little more than three years before, busying themselves with the work involved on the farm the girls' father had left Rachel. They welcomed having Violet as a part of their lives, but she always felt a little guilty about them never having time to themselves. How could she think of spoiling the first opportunity they'd had to be off on their own?

She couldn't. Pushing her qualms firmly to the back of her mind, she patted her mouth with her napkin and sent a determined smile around the table. By the time Rachel returned, the Wingate children would be settled with their new guardian and the whole episode would make an amusing tale to share. Especially if she got some rest between now and then.

Frederick folded his napkin and tucked it under the edge of his plate. "May we be excused, Miss Violet?"

"Of course." She watched the three children scamper off. "It's still light outside," she called after them. "Why don't you play outdoors a bit before bedtime?" Shrill cheers and the slam of the front door told her they approved her suggestion.

She leaned back in her chair, glad for the moment's respite. "More coffee?" At Willie's nod, she poured fresh cups for them both. She sipped her coffee and considered the man across the table from her. He hadn't made one derogatory comment during the meal. Amazing. He didn't seem so bad when he left off badmouthing the children.

Tonight he seemed preoccupied by something. Apparently he hadn't had any more success in finding Hadlock. She took another sip, taking advantage of his distraction to study him more closely. The rigors of ranch life had given him a lean, sinewy build, she noted, along with a tanned complexion from hours spent outdoors. His work-hardened hands carried the calluses of manual labor, but his easy familiarity with table manners indicated a proper upbringing.

At the moment, he had his gaze fixed on the tablecloth; but she knew if he glanced up, she'd look into eyes that matched the color of a summer sky. And that stubborn lock of hair still insisted on falling down over his forehead. She noted the wayward strands with a smile. He could almost be the knight of her imagination, if he just didn't seem to hate children so much.

Willie chose that moment to look up, and his gaze locked onto hers. A funny tingle started in the region of her stomach, then spread up into her throat. Strange, she'd felt just fine up until then. Her fingers were trembling too. She clasped her hands together, hoping Willie wouldn't notice.

Her lips parted and she pressed them together. They opened again of their own accord. Really, she ought to say something, if only to keep from looking like a gaping fish. "How did your search go today?"

Willie shook his head and the light in his eyes dimmed. "Still no sign of him. I've checked every place and every person Sheriff Dolan told me about. It's almost like the man's vanished off the face of the earth."

For the first time, Violet felt a tender concern for him. How frustrating it must be, to have left home and family on what amounted to a mission of mercy, only to find oneself stymied at every turn. She opened her mouth—intentionally, this time—to offer some consolation, when Willie continued his story.

"One good thing happened, though." A flicker of hope rekindled the spark in his eyes. "It looks like I'm going to have some help from now on."

"Really?" Violet felt a sudden surge of joy at this sign of encouragement.

"I met someone in town who knows just about everybody. Once she found out how much trouble I've had finding Hadlock, she offered to help me look for him." He brushed his forehead, pushing the errant strands of hair back into place. "Having someone local help me ask questions should make people open up more."

"Oh." Violet tried to recapture her earlier happiness for him. He had a point; getting assistance from someone who knew the lay of the land ought to prove most helpful. Sheriff Dolan didn't have time to poke around looking for Hadlock, and goodness knew her own schedule didn't allow for that. She ought to be happy for both him and the children, not feel like the proverbial dog in the manger.

"Who is it?" She tried to inject a bright note into her voice. She could sound pleased, even if she didn't feel that way.

"It's a Miss Downey." He tilted his head back to swallow the last drop of coffee. "Mary Rose Downey." He rose as if to leave, then stopped and stared at Violet. "Is anything wrong?"

"Mary Rose Downey and Thurman Hadlock." Violet forced the words out past the constriction in her throat. If he had reached across the table and slapped her, she couldn't have felt more stunned. "You do choose interesting companions, don't you?"

"Now, wait a minute!" Willie planted his hands on the table and leaned toward her. "Leaving those kids to Hadlock wasn't my idea. And I didn't ask Mary Rose to help out; she just offered. As a friendly gesture. Some people reach out to help instead of biting other people's heads off."

"And you have to accept every offer that's given, is that it?"

"If you remember," Willie shouted, "it wasn't even my idea to come out here in the first place. If my cousin had kept his guard up just a little while longer, he'd be the one out here being unappreciated, not me."

"What a shame it didn't happen that way." Violet rose to her feet and flounced across the room. "If you'll excuse me," she said, sweeping past Willie with the regal air of royalty sidestepping a minion, "I need to send the children to gather the eggs. I got so busy earlier I didn't get around to it, and there's just enough light left, if they hurry."

Willie put his hand out to stop her. "Eggs? You're letting those kids get the eggs?"

Violet raised her chin and fixed him with a lofty stare. "And why not? Don't you believe in teaching children responsibility?"

"Oh, absolutely." His mouth worked. "Yes, Ma'am, I surely do. You just go right ahead and send those little darlings after the eggs. Just stay away from doorways." He picked up his hat and exited, chuckling.

Violet stared after him. What had gotten into him? What had gotten into her, for that matter? She couldn't remember a time she'd gone from fluttery trembling to outright rudeness like that. What on earth had set her off like that? She pressed her fists against her temples, trying to recall the course of their conversation.

Oh, yes. Mary Rose Downey and her offer to help. And which bothered her most, the memory of Mary Rose or the knowledge she'd be spending time with Willie? *Be honest, Violet. Would you feel like this if a man had offered to help him?*

But he had no idea of Mary Rose's character. . .or lack of it. He'd be like a fly caught in her skillfully woven web before he knew it. And what did it matter to her? Willie Bradley was a grown man and didn't need her advice on how to run his life. He'd dropped into her neatly ordered existence out of the blue and would go out of it just as quickly. He probably wouldn't welcome her advice, anyway.

With a wistful sigh, she hooked the egg basket over her arm and went outside to call the children.

seven

Willie made his way back to his cabin, enjoying the warmer evening air. Tonight the light breeze felt almost balmy. Leaning against the side of the barn, he looked up at the darkening sky and waited for his favorite constellations to appear: Orion the Hunter with his belt of three stars and the Big and Little Dippers in their constant rotation around the North Star. In another hour, when the sky had become truly dark, the faint cluster of the Seven Sisters would be visible in the East.

As children, he and Lizzie spent hours staring at the stars each evening. His sister might even be looking at them right now, he thought. With the supper dishes cleaned up and put away, maybe she and Adam sat on their broad front porch at that very moment, watching the timeless display.

He entered his cabin and lit the lamp, his meager furnishings becoming visible when the match flared up. For some reason he couldn't begin to name, he felt more content than he'd been in a long time. His circumstances had changed dramatically over the past few weeks, but he saw the same stars tonight he would have seen at home in New Mexico. The God who created them—and him—was as present with him here as back at the ranch. He sat on the edge of his cot and pulled off one of his boots.

For the first time since leaving home, he measured his problems against the backdrop of the heavens' grandeur and saw them as small indeed. Surely he could trust the Creator of the universe to solve his minor troubles. Even a trio of Wingates didn't pose too big a problem for the Almighty.

The reminder of the children caused him to stop in the act of tugging off his other boot. Violet had sent them to get eggs, and he hadn't given her much in the way of a word of caution.

62

He should have warned her about Frederick's egg trick.

Nah, let her find out on her own just how adorable those three can be. He chuckled and undid the buttons on his work shirt, wondering just how long it would be before they showed their true colors.

Why would anyone in their right mind volunteer to take on those hoodlums in training? He pulled his shirt over his head and hung it on a peg, turning the question over in his mind. He knew firsthand how disarming the trio could be at first sight; he'd been bamboozled himself, until he spent time alone with them. Understandable, then, that a tender heart like Violet's would feel sympathy for them in the beginning.

But after spending days on end in their company? It didn't make sense.

Willie ran his fingers through his hair and prepared to stretch out on the thin mattress. He'd posed that puzzle to Mary Rose earlier in the day, while they walked down the boardwalk, her dainty hand tucked trustingly in the crook of his arm.

He closed his eyes and inhaled, as if he could bring back the scent of lilac water that surrounded her in a fragrant cloud. Unlike Violet, she hadn't despised him on sight. In fact, she'd seemed pretty impressed by his description of his home and family. And she'd patted his arm in consolation when he related his misadventures in trying to connect the Wingate children with their new home. Overall, her frank admiration and sympathy bolstered his badly wounded pride and made Willie feel like a hero.

"And you say Violet Canfield is caring for them?" Mary Rose fluttered eyelashes like fans in his direction. "Is she an old friend of your family? Or the children's, perhaps?"

Willie shook his head. "Not at all. I'd never seen her in my life before I tracked the kids to her door."

"And she agreed, just like that, when you asked her to care for children didn't know?"

"I didn't ask; she told me that's how it was going to be."

Willie flushed at the memory. "At the time, it didn't set real well with me; but I have to admit, it's all worked out for the best. I've been able to spend my time looking for Hadlock without the three of them underfoot." No need to add that he wouldn't have been able to squire a certain young lady along the streets of Prescott if the kids had been his to watch.

"But I still can't figure out why she keeps on doing it. I know what those kids are like. Either they've done a grand job of keeping her fooled, or she has more grit than I gave her credit for."

"Or maybe she thinks it's worth her while to put up with them in spite of all their mischief." Mary Rose looked up at him with speculative green eyes. "Money, perhaps?"

Willie knew the start he gave answered her question before he ever opened his mouth. "They do stand to inherit a fair amount," he said slowly, remembering the sum Monroe had mentioned. "But she'd have no way of knowing that."

Mary Rose laughed again and gave his arm a playful swat. "Men can be so innocent," she teased. "She had plenty of time to cozy up to them and learn every little detail long before you showed up. Maybe there really is more to Violet than that delicate exterior she shows to the world."

Mary Rose's words swirled through Willie's head while he lay on his cot, arms pillowing his head. Could it be true? Did Violet know about the Wingate money and have plans to latch onto it if Hadlock couldn't be found? Even given their unending friction, he wouldn't have thought it of her; but women knew other women, or so he'd always heard.

Did Mary Rose know something about Violet he didn't? She hadn't said she disliked Violet in so many words, but her tone carried that implication clearly enough. And Violet's reaction to his mention of Mary Rose at the supper table made her feelings about the other woman abundantly clear. It didn't take a genius to see the two women shared a mutual lack of regard. But did either of them have a valid reason? As far as he could see, neither had a solid basis for their attitude.

He frowned into the darkness, trying to assess the situation. It seemed clear that Mary Rose's offer of help came purely from the goodness of her heart; there could be no other motive. And only that morning, he would have sworn Violet's affection for the children was genuine, if misguided. He hadn't seen a thing to make him believe otherwise.

Until Mary Rose put the thought into his mind. Willie sat up and combed his fingers through his tousled hair, then yanked his shirt on over his head and stepped into his boots. He wouldn't sleep a wink until he knew for sure whether Violet had heard about the kids' inheritance.

Lights still burned inside the house. Good. If everyone had already gone to bed, he'd have had to turn back and stay awake all night, chewing on the question. He rapped on the front door and drew back, startled, when Jessica answered his knock.

"Miss Violet's putting Toby to bed," she told him. "My turn's next."

Willie responded with an unwilling grin. Jessica's blond hair streamed down her back in silky waves. Bare toes peeked out from under the hem of her white nightdress. If he didn't have all too much insight into her true nature, she'd look awfully cute. Could it be that Violet's loving care had given the kids sufficient motivation to mend their ways? Maybe they'd decided to settle down and behave. If they did, it would sure make his job easier.

No point in carrying a grudge; if they were willing to turn around, he could meet them halfway. He knelt down in front of the little girl to put himself at her eye level. "Do you think she'd have time to talk to me when she's finished?"

Jessica smiled and nodded. "Probably."

Willie's heart warmed. When she wasn't plotting or carrying out some nefarious scheme, she could be one little charmer. He started to speak, ready to draw out their conversation, when approaching footsteps caught his attention.

"Did I hear someone at the door?" Violet walked into the room and stopped short at the sight of Willie. He rose to his feet, suddenly self-conscious about the question he'd come to ask.

"It's just me," he said, adding with a grin at his small companion, "Jessica and I were having a little chat."

Jessica drew herself up ramrod straight and took two steps backward. "And I don't care what you say," she huffed, "I don't believe Miss Violet would ever do a thing like that." She flounced off toward the rear of the house without a backward glance.

Violet stared at him wide-eyed. "And may I ask just what you've been telling her about me?" She advanced on him, fists on her hips and fire smoldering in the gaze she turned on him.

He opened and closed his mouth, but no sound came forth. He swallowed hard. "I have no idea," he managed to say.

Violet raised a disbelieving eyebrow. "Surely you can do better than that."

"So help me, all I'd done was ask whether you could spare the time to talk to me."

"And I'm supposed to believe she came up with a remark like that on her own?" The look she gave him could have withered a small oak at twenty yards. "I'd been foolish enough to think you were finished casting aspersions on the children."

"Well, no— I mean—" Willie clamped his lips together. He sounded like a moron, even to himself.

Violet fixed him with a haughty gaze. "Did you have something specific you wanted to discuss, or did you just come by to talk about me behind my back?"

"I was going to ask you—" He broke off, knowing full well how his question would sound in light of their current conversation.

He gulped and tried again. Hadn't he already made enough mess of things for one night? Nothing could make him look much worse in her eyes than he did already. . .unless it was the question he was about to ask. Still, he had to know.

"Do you know anything about the money the kids are going to come into?" There, it was out. He waited for the roof to cave in. To his amazement, Violet threw back her head and laughed.

"You mean their inheritance?" At Willie's dumbfounded nod, she chortled again. "Yes, the little scamps told me all about the money their father left them. I suppose they thought it might make them look more important, poor little things. As if they needed to do something to impress me. But you needn't worry that I took them seriously."

"But—"

"How on earth did they manage to come up with such a fanciful story?" Violet tilted her head to one side and cast a quizzical glance at Willie. "To think a wild tale like that could come from the imaginations of such young children. What put it in their heads, do you suppose?"

Willie's mind reeled. "You don't believe it then?"

Violet shook her head and gave him a pitying smile. "How could I? It's hardly logical. If their father had that kind of means, would he have chosen someone like Thurman Hadlock as their guardian?" She erupted once more into peals of laughter.

"I guess that would be hard to figure, wouldn't it?" Willie attempted a grin and edged toward the porch steps. "Well, that was all I wanted to ask you. Good night."

The soft smile left Violet's lips and her stern expression returned. "Please don't try to malign the children again. You're much more likable, you know, when you don't tell stories about them."

Willie's foot slipped, and he saved himself from a fall only by twisting his body into wild contortions between the top step and the ground. Behind him he heard a soft giggle before Violet closed the door. Within minutes he had regained the solitude of his cabin and once more stretched out on the cot.

"What do You think about that, Lord?" he whispered. "She'll believe any crazy story those kids make up about me, but she doesn't recognize the truth when it up and stares her in the face. I know You created women, so You must understand them. But it sure is a tough proposition for the rest of us."

He laced his fingers behind his head and considered the other women he'd known. That pretty much narrowed the field down to his mother, his sister, and his aunt, all basically normal females. True, his mother seemed to have gone a bit softheaded with the advent of her first grandchild; but in her usual state, she had plenty of common sense. If she hadn't been so addled by Lizzie's coming confinement and the arrival of Cousin Lewis, he knew she'd never have been taken in by the Wingate tribe, sweet faces or no.

What about Lizzie? She had been Willie's closest friend and playmate all through their growing-up years. He knew her almost as well as he knew himself. *It's a pity she couldn't get over to visit before I left,* he mused. *She would have seen right through those three.*

On the other hand, every woman they'd run across in their travels to Prescott seemed to feel an immediate need to take on a protective role toward the children. Even when it meant protecting them from him. It just proved his point: There was no figuring women.

So where did that put Violet? If he'd met her under different circumstances, unencumbered and Wingate-free, they might have started off on better footing. Her delicate figure and graceful walk were enough to catch a man's notice right off. With the addition of glossy sable hair framing her heart-shaped face, it made for a stunning combination.

And those eyes! Willie pursed his lips in a silent whistle. He'd seen plenty of blue eyes in his family. He had blue eyes himself. So did his father, Uncle Jeff, Aunt Judith, and his cousins. But *these.* . . He'd never encountered the likes of them before. Blue as a delphinium, blue as the hottest part of a flame. With their intensity, they could scorch a man or melt his heart. He'd met a beauty, no doubt about it.

But what went on beneath that lovely exterior? He reflected on this dilemma, fighting off the drowsiness that made his eyelids drift closed despite his attempts to keep them open. She didn't seem like an empty-headed dreamer, but to all appearances she'd been taken in hook, line, and sinker by every story the kids had told her, save the one about the money their father had left them. *Funny,* he mused, *that she missed the truth about that one.*

Or had she? The thought jolted him wide awake. What if that slim body housed a devious brain, one that did indeed recognize the inheritance story as the truth and had decided to benefit from it?

Could lovely Violet be capable of such duplicity? The thought gnawed at him, and sleep fled.

eight

"Miss Violet, I don't feel so good."

Violet scooped the last of the scrambled eggs from the frying pan onto a serving dish and set it on the table next to the platter of bacon. "What's wrong, Honey?" She turned back to the counter and sliced a freshly baked loaf of bread with smooth, practiced strokes.

"My throat hurts."

"Probably from talking too much." Willie's comment, though mumbled, carried clearly.

Violet swung around and pointed the bread knife at him. "I thought we had an agreement."

He raised his hands in surrender. "You're right. I apologize." His sullen demeanor didn't match his words, but she decided to let it go. Might as well take any concession he was willing to give.

She handed the bread plate to Frederick and circled the table to lay her hand on Jessica's forehead. A flutter of concern knotted her stomach.

"Willie." Even to her own ears, her voice sounded strange.

He paused in the act of loading his breakfast plate and looked up. A frown creased his forehead when he met her gaze. "What's wrong?"

"I need you to go into town and fetch the doctor." She could hear her voice rising, tight with fear. She cleared her throat before she continued, hoping to inject a more casual note into her tone. "Since you're going in for supplies, anyway, it won't take but a few moments extra. His office is right over the mercantile." There, that sounded much calmer.

"Fine." His face cleared and he picked up his fork. "I'll head out as soon as I've finished eating."

Maybe she'd sounded too calm. She spooned a mound of eggs from his plate onto a slice of bread, laid two strips of bacon across the eggs, and piled another slice of bread on top, ignoring his startled yip. "Here. You can eat this on the way." When he opened his mouth to protest, she shook her head and laid her finger across her lips, nodding toward the door. She breathed a sigh of relief when he followed her out onto the kitchen stoop without further argument.

"She's running a fever," she told him. "A high one. You need to leave as soon as you can get the horse hitched up." She shoved the improvised sandwich into his hands.

"Hurry," she pleaded. "I'm truly worried about her."

Willie responded with a gratifying air of concern and hurried toward the barn. Violet returned to the kitchen, where the two boys mopped up the remains of the bacon and eggs with their bread and Jessica stared listlessly at her untouched plate.

Violet put an arm around the little girl and helped her out of her chair. "Come on, Jessie. Let's get you back to bed."

"She just got up," Toby argued around a mouthful of eggs.

"Things are a little different this morning. You boys help yourselves to seconds, if you'd like." She scooped Jessie into her arms and hastened down the hall.

In the bedroom, she helped Jessie out of her pinafore and into her nightdress and tied her hair back with a ribbon. After tucking the little girl in bed, she hurried to the kitchen and returned with a cloth and a basin of water.

"This should make you feel better." She sponged Jessie's forehead with the cool water, remembering how Rachel had once cared for her the same way during a bout with influenza. "Does that help any?"

Jessie closed her eyes and tossed her head in fretful denial. Moist wisps of her wheat-colored hair clung to her forehead. Violet smoothed them back with her fingertips and winced at the heat emanating from the little girl's body. If only the doctor would arrive! She stared at the small form on the bed and felt her throat tighten. No matter how her heart had gone out to her animal patients in the past, this was far different than taking care of a bird or a squirrel, and the stakes were much higher. For the first time during one of her rescue efforts, Violet felt burdened by a sense of inadequacy.

She dipped the cloth in the basin again, this time wiping Jessie's arms and hands. Jessie whimpered and pulled away. Violet studied the little girl. Heat from the fever had added color to her fair complexion, almost as if. . . Padding across the floor so as not to disturb the sick child, she pulled the curtain back to admit the morning sun. Light filled the room and washed across the bed. She peered at Jessie's face.

"Honey, were you outside without your bonnet yesterday? It looks like the sun has burned your poor little face."

Jessica murmured an unintelligible reply. Violet resumed her seat at the bedside and continued bathing her face and arms. She'd had sunburns herself, enough to turn her nose pink and even make it peel at times, but she'd never gotten sick from it. She'd never been burned as badly as Jessie seemed to be, though.

Remorse smote her. She ought to have noticed whether or not the child had worn her bonnet. Jessie's fair skin was no match for the intense northern Arizona sun. Why had she let yesterday's turmoil keep her from fulfilling her responsibility? If she hadn't been so caught up in talk of Mary Rose Downey and its aftermath, she *would* have noticed. She felt sure of that.

Don't let anything bad happen to Jessie because I wasn't paying attention, Lord. Help me know what to do.

An overwhelming weariness swept through her. How did mothers manage to take care of the myriad details of housekeeping plus tend to their children's needs and watch out for their safety? It seemed so simple on the surface, but carrying it out proved to be another matter altogether. Her shoulders settled against the back of the chair. Her eyelids drifted shut, and she dropped her hands into her lap. It felt so good to relax for just a moment.

A light breeze drifted in through the window, and Violet roused with a start when she heard the voices of her two other charges. How could she have forgotten about them? She shook her head to clear it and glanced at Jessie. The little girl appeared to be asleep. Violet noted her steady breathing and felt reassured. Satisfied her absence wouldn't be noticed for a time, she rose, grimacing at the damp coolness on her lap. She'd dropped the cloth without noticing when she became drowsy, and now a large circle marred the front of her skirt.

No matter. She had more important concerns at the moment than the state of her clothes. She hurried outdoors to see what the boys were doing. On second thought, she retrieved their hats from the hooks in their room and carried them with her. No point in risking any more sunburns.

Stupid! Willie berated himself all during the wagon ride into town. Just how much of an idiot could one man be? As if he needed to add to the black marks on his slate from the night before, he had to go and make that snide comment about Jessica's sore throat being caused by too much talking.

The memory of it made him want to bite his tongue. For all their perfidy, the Wingates were only little kids; but he was a grown man, supposedly able to control his tongue and keep his temper in check. *What's wrong with me, Lord? Haven't I heard those verses about a gentle answer turning away wrath often enough?*

Violet's concern for Jessica's health had been evident in the way her voice tightened and her hands trembled. And what had he done? Only added to her worries by his thoughtless quip. Hopefully, his quick departure once she made the situation clear had reassured her that he could be more of a gentleman than he'd shown her up to now.

He clucked to the horse to pick up the pace. The sorrel gelding could rest while he ran his errands in town. Right now, the important thing was to find that doctor and get him started on his way. Where did Violet say his office was located? He spied the gilt lettering—Phineas Hathaway, M.D.—on the door above the mercantile and set the wagon brake.

With the doctor alerted, Willie felt free to go about his business. Jessica did have a fever, he reasoned, but surely it would turn out to be nothing more than a bad cold or some other innocuous complaint.

An hour later, Willie looked at the wagonload of supplies with satisfaction. He decided to take just a few more minutes in town and turned his steps toward the telegraph office. A sweet voice called his name just as he reached the door. He looked back over his shoulder and saw a smiling Mary Rose heading his way.

He felt a broad grin spread over his face. Maybe the day wouldn't turn out to be a total loss after all. Mary Rose's company could take a load of care off a man in a hurry.

The scent of lilacs wafted toward him when she approached. "I didn't know whether I'd ever see you again," she pouted, tucking her hand into the crook of his arm in a proprietary gesture that made his heart race. "I thought you might have finished your business here and gone off to that ranch of yours without another thought for poor little me."

Willie's mouth went dry as a drought-parched pasture. Did it really matter to a lovely woman like Mary Rose whether she saw him again or not? They had only met a bare twenty-four hours before, after all. He peered at her more closely and saw her lower lip quiver. The sight stirred a feeling of protectiveness, and he pressed a reassuring hand over her fingertips.

The smile she turned on him could have lit up the whole town on a moonless night. Willie nodded toward the office doors. "I was just going to see if I'd had a reply to a telegram I sent home. Would you care to join me?"

"Only if you'll join me for a cup of tea when you've finished your business here." Her inviting gaze made his heart lurch.

Monroe's response to Willie's query about bringing the children home until he could return with them himself was succinct and to the point. The word <u>NO</u> sat alone in the center of the yellow paper, leaving no room for doubt.

Willie thanked the clerk, folded the missive, and tucked it into his coat pocket, surprised at how little the abrupt refusal disturbed him. Somehow with Mary Rose clinging to his arm, staying around Prescott a while longer didn't seem like such a bad idea. Not to mention the prospect of another train trip with the three Wingates no longer hung over his head.

He passed a pleasant half hour drinking tea with Mary Rose, then walked her to her home once again and went on his way. Recounting her every word, look, and gesture filled the drive back to the farm in a most pleasant manner.

He started into the curve leading to the farm and turned his horse to the side to avoid the buckboard that rattled along the road toward him. The grizzled driver pulled on the reins and studied him. His face broke into a broad smile, revealing several missing teeth.

"You must be the young feller with all the kids who's staying here with Violet."

Willie stared at the scruffy newcomer. "I guess that would be me," he agreed slowly.

The other man beamed. "Thought so." He held out a calloused hand. "Put 'er there. My name's Jeb McCurdy. I live just down the road." He pointed a gnarled finger over his shoulder.

"Willie Bradley." He returned the older man's grip, surprised at its strength. McCurdy seemed in no hurry to leave. He might as well question him while he had the opportunity. "I'm looking for a man named Thurman Hadlock. Do you know him?"

The benevolent glow faded from McCurdy's eyes. "I should say I do. What do you want with him? You don't look like the sort he usually hangs out with."

After learning something of Hadlock's reputation, Willie felt glad to hear that. "He's been named guardian of the children. I've come to take them to him."

McCurdy shook his head somberly. "I don't know where he is, and if I did, I'm not sure I'd tell you. That man doesn't have a decent bone in his body." Then he brightened. "Tell you what. You stop by my place one of these days and we'll figure out someone else who can take those kids. How about it?"

Willie chuckled at the earnest offer. "We'll see, Jeb. At any rate, it's been nice talking to you."

"Likewise," his neighbor said. He picked up the reins and shook them. "Come see me if you get in a bind."

Willie nudged his horse forward and continued around the curve. He frowned in surprise when he saw the doctor's buggy still standing in front of the house and the doctor himself busy nailing a brightly colored placard to the gate post.

"What's going on?" he called, as soon as he was within earshot.

Doc Hathaway pounded in the final nail before taking any notice of Willie's presence. "I'm putting the place under quarantine," he told him brusquely. "I'm afraid young Jessica has scarlet fever."

"Scarlet. . . But she seemed fine yesterday. All she said this morning was that her throat hurt."

The doctor nodded. "That's how it often begins. By the time I arrived, the rash had already started on her face and spread to her neck. Right now she's one sick little girl."

"How about the boys? They don't have it, do they?"

"Not yet, but with as much close contact as family members have, there's a good chance they'll catch it from her." He dusted his hands together and shook his head. "Violet's going to have her hands full."

"Surely some of the neighbors or people from town. . ." Willie's voice trailed off when the doctor tapped the quarantine notice.

"I don't want this spreading if I can help it. No one but me goes in or out past this sign until further notice."

Indecision tore at Willie. The idea of staying cooped up with Violet and the kids for an indeterminate period held all the appeal of building a mile of fence singlehandly, especially when it would put an end to his search for Hadlock for all that time. He eyed the provisions in the wagon bed. Surely he could unload them on the porch, unhitch the wagon, and hightail it back to town without the doctor objecting. They'd have plenty of food, and he could continue looking for the elusive guardian without interruption.

An image of Violet flashed into his mind, and he remembered the dark circles under her eyes that morning, her drooping shoulders, and the worry etched on her face. Tempting as it might be to be shed of the kids for awhile, he couldn't subject her to caring for the three of them without help. And what would happen if she came down with the disease herself, leaving her at the mercy of those renegades? The recollection of Monroe's fractured leg made up his mind for him.

He clicked his tongue and urged the horse past the gate. "I'm staying," he told the bushy-browed doctor. "I picked up supplies this morning, so we'll be set for however long it takes. We'll be fine." He hoped he could live up to that brave assurance.

Doc Hathaway stiffened and fixed him with a stern gaze, then relaxed, apparently reassured by what he saw. He dipped his head in reluctant acquiescence. "I'll say this to your face: I'd be more inclined to horsewhip you than let you stay if I hadn't already heard about you from the sheriff. Dolan's a good man. If he vouches for you, I guess you're all right."

The halfhearted compliment sent a jolt of unexpected encouragement through Willie. Dolan had stopped by a time or two to see how his search was progressing. They'd spent time talking and seemed to get along all right, but he had no idea the sheriff had formed such a positive opinion of him. Coming from a man like Dolan, the accolade meant a lot.

Doc stepped up into his buggy and picked up the reins. "I'll look in later," he promised. "If you need anything from town, nail a list to the gate post and McCurdy can pick them up for you." He flicked the buggy whip and drove away.

Willie stopped the horse at the foot of the porch steps and started unloading bags and boxes. He looked at the pile of supplies, gauging how long they would last. Realization struck him with a sense of finality: As long as the quarantine lasted, they wouldn't be able to count on anyone else's presence or help. If the boys contracted the disease one after the other, it might be a month before he could leave the farm again.

nine

"It tastes good, Miss Violet." Jessie smiled, the first sign of animation Violet had seen in her since she'd taken sick.

"I'm glad, Honey. You need to keep eating so you can get better." Violet spooned the last of the chicken broth into the little girl's mouth, then set the bowl on the bedside table. She dipped the cloth into the basin and sponged Jessica's forehead.

"That feels so nice," the little girl murmured, her voice slurred with drowsiness. Her eyelids batted once, then twice, then drifted shut and stayed that way.

Violet continued bathing her head and arms, hoping her ministrations would help bring that high temperature down soon. When her arms tired, she sat watching Jessie's chest rise and fall with her breathing, giving a quick little catch from time to time. Damp ringlets of wheat-colored hair clung to the little girl's forehead, and Violet brushed them back tenderly, trying not to waken the sleeping child.

Surely this wouldn't last much longer. When the rash she'd mistaken for sunburn started to spread from Jessie's face to her chest and back, then her arms and legs, Violet had been able to do nothing but watch the disease's progress with horror. . .and prayer. Thank the Lord, it had begun to fade, although red streaks remained in the creases under her arms and inside the crook of her elbows. Those would go away soon, according to what Doc Hathaway said on his visit earlier that afternoon.

"You've done a fine job," he said in his gravelly voice. "If all my patients had the diligent care you've given this little sprite, my job would be a lot easier." He pulled his stethoscope from around his neck and placed it back in his medical bag. "With the rash fading like it is, you can expect her fever to go away in

79

another day or so. Once that happens, she should begin to recover quickly."

Violet felt a surge of hope for the first time in the days since his first visit to Jessie. "Does that mean you'll remove the quarantine sign soon?"

The doctor picked up his bag and pursed his lips in thought, skewing his bristly white mustache to one side. He shook his head. "It stays in place. Nobody goes in or out of here but me. This little scamp is doing well—" He tweaked Jessie's toes through the comforter, eliciting a weak giggle from the sick girl. "—but I don't want to risk having an outbreak on my hands. I look for the boys to come down with it anytime within the next few days. We'll see what happens then.

"In the meantime. . ." He turned to Violet and wagged a finger under her nose. "You take better care of yourself, young lady. That means plenty of food and plenty of rest. I won't have you jeopardizing your own health. Do you understand?"

Violet essayed a bright smile of agreement and kept it fixed on her face until the sound of the front door closing told her the doctor had gone and she could safely slump against the bedstead in despair.

Fine for him to tell her to eat and sleep, she reflected, wearily dipping the cloth in the basin and beginning the sponging procedure once more. He didn't have to worry about two lively boys in addition to their sick sister. He didn't have to plan meals, clean the house, and do the laundry.

He didn't have to find time to prepare meals for three hearty male appetites on top of fixing the nourishing soups and pots of strong tea he'd recommended for Jessie. And that didn't include the time spent cajoling the reluctant child to allow Violet to spoon tea and soup down her throat.

He didn't have to find time to take care of personal needs in the midst of the multitude of chores that faced her.

Speaking of chores. . . She heaved herself out of the chair. She gathered up the bowl and cup and tiptoed out of the room.

Unwashed dishes, unscrubbed counter, unswept floor. Violet surveyed the disaster in the kitchen through fatigue-dulled eyes. Willie and the boys had taken over the outdoor chores, and she would ever be grateful for that, but the housework still fell to her, and she didn't know how she'd begin to catch up.

With a weary sigh, she placed Jessie's empty bowl atop the pile of dirty dishes and ladled out some soup for herself. She swallowed two spoonfuls, then set the bowl aside. With all the responsibility she carried these days, who had the time or energy to eat? She leaned against the counter and propped up her forehead with one hand. Even before Jessie's illness, she'd had the uneasy feeling she might have bitten off more than she could chew. Today she felt as though her myriad duties were choking her.

Violet forced her exhausted body upright and began to stack the dishes in the sink. If she didn't make a dent in this mess soon, there wouldn't be a clean dish left in the house. Her eyes brimmed with unbidden tears. She felt tired, more tired than she could ever remember being in her life, even during that awful period just after Pa's death when she and Rachel had been forced to run the farm on their own. Not only did she have the physical chores to do; the sheer responsibility of keeping tabs on the children and ensuring their safety weighed on her like an anvil.

Despite the relief their departure would bring, she dreaded the day Willie located Thurman Hadlock. The specter of his guardianship never left her mind for long.

How would the three children she had grown to love fare under his dubious care? Try as she might, she could only envision a grim future for them. Nearly as grim as the prospect of Rachel's imminent return. Violet could only imagine what her sister would say when she found her home had been taken over by strangers. Such thoughts were best left alone. Reality would come soon enough. Any hope that the Wingate family would have relocated to their new home by the time Rachel and Daniel returned had flown out the window with the onset of Jessie's illness.

She placed the last of the cups on top of the towering pile. Just having the crockery arranged in a more orderly heap made a definite improvement to the appearance of the room, and Violet's spirits rose accordingly. As soon as she drew water and heated it, she could start on the actual cleanup. She lifted the bucket from its place and made it halfway to the door before her knees threatened to buckle. She swayed and wiped her forehead with the back of her hand.

What had come over her? Going out to draw a bucket of water seemed a small enough task. Goodness knew, she'd done the same chore countless times before. But today, she simply couldn't face the simple act. Feeling like a lazy quitter, she replaced the bucket and stumbled back to the sickroom. She would have to wash the dishes later. Right now, she just didn't have the strength.

She sagged into the chair at Jessie's bedside, willing herself to keep her spine erect and not lean back against the cushions. If she relaxed even that much, she knew she'd never be able to remain awake.

Her thoughts drifted back to Rachel and her probable reaction when she came home. Maybe she should have mentioned something about her current situation in a letter, just to prepare her sister for the children's presence. Not to mention Willie's.

What would her sister think when she discovered a strange man had been living on their property? Violet shuddered at the prospect. Rachel would not be pleased, not at all. She afforded herself the tiny luxury of letting her shoulder blades make contact with the back of the chair. She could allow that much comfort and still be able to remain alert.

She would have to convince Rachel of Willie's upright character. That wouldn't be the insurmountable task it would have seemed when they first met, she reflected. Willie had lost a lot of his aggravating ways. And thank goodness he had chosen to stay, or she never would have been able to cope. She would not soon forget the relief that swept over her when she found out he'd chosen to share the quarantine of his own free will. She didn't want to contemplate what would have happened had she been left to handle all three children completely on her own.

Not for the first time, Violet wondered whether she'd done a terribly foolish thing in taking on such a huge responsibility. Tending to her former animal patients had used up only an hour or two of her day. It hadn't taken long for her to realize that caring for a human child involved a whole different level of commitment, one she didn't know if she could handle much longer. Could she live up to the trust the children and Doc Hathaway placed in her?

It would be different once Rachel got back and she had a little help. She let her head rest against the tufted cushion, then shook it impatiently. How could she think of asking her sister to assume a workload like this when she hadn't had a thing to do with inviting a crew of strange children and their irascible escort to stay? This wasn't Rachel's responsibility. It was hers, Violet's, and she would handle it on her own.

If she could just get some rest, she'd be able to manage. Her chin sagged, and she nodded, then jerked her head up with a start. She didn't dare nap now. Too many chores awaited her. But surely a few moments relaxation wouldn't hurt. She let her head slip back against the chair once more and let out a blissful sigh. She didn't have to go to sleep; she could simply sit still and enjoy a brief respite. Then she'd be able to pull herself up and go on. Just a few blessed minutes. . .

Her eyelids fluttered, then closed.

ten

"Want me to throw the hay down?"

Willie looked at Frederick, already halfway up the ladder to the hayloft, and shook his head. "I'll do it." He waited for the disgruntled youngster to descend, then climbed up and tossed forkfuls of hay to the two boys below. *Give one of them the advantage of height? And equip him with a pitchfork? No, thank you.*

He watched the brothers gather up the hay and carry it to the manger. He had to admit they'd done pretty well at keeping up with him while he split wood, fed the livestock, and milked the cow. Not many complaints, either, and not a single attempt at a practical joke. But he couldn't quite bring himself to let down his guard completely, not after what they'd put him through. He descended the ladder rungs and helped the boys throw the last of the hay to the milk cow.

"That's it for tonight, Fellas. You put in a good day's work." Might as well give them credit when he could. Maybe it would inspire them to live up to a higher standard. He took a last look around the barn, then carried the lantern to the doorway and waited for the boys to exit so he could swing the heavy doors shut for the night. Instead, they stood unmoving, their faces solemn in the lantern's dim glow.

They looked at each other as though passing some kind of silent communication between them, then turned to Willie. "Can we ask you something?" Frederick's voice sounded a faint echo in the barn's shadowy interior.

Willie's stomach clenched. Had they managed to set up some kind of trap without his seeing them? "Sure." He strode back to join them, keeping a careful watch for hidden snares. He stopped just short of the boys, holding the lantern high so as to get a clear look at them. "What is it?"

Again the boys exchanged glances, then Toby looked up to meet Willie's gaze. "What happens when you die?" The question hung suspended on the night air.

Willie bent down to scrutinize the small boy's face, seeing the worried puckers in the lamplight. "Any special reason you're asking?" he queried, hoping he'd just come up against a normal childish query and that the inquiry hadn't been prompted by any plans the two might have made for his immediate future.

Toby's chin quivered, and he clapped a grimy hand over his mouth. Frederick took up the line of questioning. "We were wondering about Jessie. Is she going to die?" Two pairs of somber eyes stared into Willie's face with an intensity that put to rest any doubts about the sincerity of their question.

Willie hung the lantern from a nail and dropped to one knee to put himself on their level. "Listen to me," he commanded, placing a hand on each boy's shoulder. "Your sister is sick, I'll grant you that. But the doctor's been in to see her every day, and he's satisfied with the way she's coming along. She's not going to die."

"But they only put up quarantine signs for really bad things." Frederick's voice came out in a quaver, despite his attempts to sound manly.

"You're right. Scarlet fever is nothing to fool around with, and the doctor doesn't want any more people catching it than he can help. That's why the sign is out there, to protect the rest of the people around here. Miss Violet's watching over Jessie every minute; you know that. She's taking good care of your sister so she can be up and around again and playing with both of you in no time."

He searched the two young faces for signs that they believed him, but their expressions still registered fear. A sudden thought came to Willie. "Did they hang out a quarantine sign when your pa took sick?"

Frederick nodded. "They hung it up when he got sick, just

like with Jessie, and Papa died." He swallowed hard and his Adam's apple bobbed in his throat.

Willie's grip on their shoulders tightened. "I still have my ma and pa, but I know what it's like to worry when one of them is sick. You've all been through a lot, but I promise you, you can quit worrying now. Jessie is going to be just fine."

"Cross your heart?" Toby asked, his voice muffled by his fingers.

Willie flinched at hearing the phrase but made a show of drawing an X on his chest with his finger. His heart swelled with relief at the flicker of acceptance he saw in their eyes, and he got to his feet, ready to walk them to the house. The boys didn't follow.

Toby pulled his hand away from his mouth. "But we still want to know," he told Willie. "What happens when you die?"

Willie knelt again, then settled back on his heel. It looked like this discussion might take some time. He cleared his throat, trying to decide what to say to the two youngsters. Just how much would they be able to understand? Plenty, he reminded himself. He'd only been about Frederick's age when he decided he wanted to belong to God's family, and Lizzie had been even younger. They could understand all they needed to. Maybe he ought to find out first just how much they did know, so he'd know where to start.

"What do you think happens?"

Toby sat cross-legged in front of him, and Frederick followed suit. "My teacher says you become an angel," Frederick confided with a hopeful gleam in his eye. "She said our ma's an angel now. I guess that means Papa is too. Is that right?"

Willie passed his hand across his face. This was going to be even harder than he thought. How did you tell two little boys something that might shake their hope for their parents' destiny? You told them the truth. "Not exactly," he began. "If you go to heaven, there are angels there, but the angels weren't people first. Understand?" Two blank faces told him he'd missed the mark. He took a deep breath and prepared to try again.

"Look," he said, trying to remember how his parents had explained it to him when he was younger, "it's like this. Everyone does bad things sometimes, right?" Both blond heads nodded in sober agreement. "Well, God calls those bad things sin. And since God can't be around sin, He can't be around us when we've sinned. Are you with me so far?"

Toby's face puckered in bemused concentration, but he didn't say a word. Frederick eyed him intently. "So if God's in heaven and if we want to go to heaven, we can't if we do wrong things?"

"That's the idea."

Frederick studied the toes of his shoes. "But if everyone does bad things," he said, shredding a piece of straw into slivers, "how does anyone get to heaven?"

Willie grinned and relaxed. The hardest part was over; from here on out, he felt on familiar ground. "That's where Jesus comes in." He paused. "You have heard of Jesus, haven't you?"

Toby swiped his sleeve across his nose. "The baby in the manger at Christmas time?"

"Well, yes. But that was when He first came to earth. Jesus is God's Son, and God sent Him here to tell people how to get right with Him. You see, He knows how people are and how we just can't always do the right things no matter how hard we try."

Frederick leaned forward, lips parted. "So how do we get to heaven if we can't do right on our own?"

Willie's heart pounded. Could it be possible that one or both boys were ready to make the decision to turn their lives over to the Lord right here and now? "We trust in Jesus. Like I said, He came to earth from heaven and never did anything wrong in His whole life."

"Not even once?" Toby's face twisted in amazement at the idea of such a feat.

"Not once." Willie's face softened into a smile. "He loved us so much, He took our punishment for us when He died on the cross. If we trust in what He did, God looks at us as though we're just as perfect as Jesus."

Frederick leaned back, his face a mask of skepticism. "That's all we have to do, say we trust Him?"

"Well, it's more than just giving Him lip service. You show you really trust Him by giving Him control of your life." He paused and wet his lips. "So what do you think, boys? Do you want to pray and ask Him to save you right now?" *Lord, please don't let me ruin this.*

A lengthy pause ensued. Willie continued to send up prayers of intercession. Toby looked at Frederick; Frederick stared at the floor, frowning fiercely. Finally, he raised his head and met Willie's gaze. "Not right now. It's too much to figure out all in one night." His face pinched in worry. "Is that all right?"

"It's okay," Willie told him, fighting down his sense of disappointment. "It wouldn't do you a bit of good to say the words if you didn't really mean them. But I want you to keep thinking about what I've said, will you promise me that?"

Frederick considered this for a moment, then nodded. "I will," he said. "Something like that is too important not to think about a lot. Right?"

"Right." Willie reached out and tousled the boy's hair, realizing it was the first friendly gesture he'd made toward any of the Wingates since their first meeting. The knowledge smote him with shame. These kids had been through the loss of both parents, plus being uprooted and hauled out West to be raised by a total stranger. That would be enough to make anyone cut up a bit.

This time the boys followed him readily when he left the barn and swung the wide door shut. He shepherded them back to the house, where he oversaw their washing up and their preparations for bed. Before blowing out the lamp in their bedroom, he stopped to lay his hand on each boy's head and say a gentle good night. Maybe all they needed was to be shown a little godly love.

What if no one had cared enough to show a loving concern

for him and tell him about God's great gift in his younger years? For the first time, he began to grasp just how blessed his upbringing had been. Not only his parents, but his aunt and uncle, too, had lived out a faithful model of God's sacrificial love in their every action toward him.

Even with their good example, his path hadn't been without its pitfalls. He remembered uneasily how, only a few years before, he had rebelled against his upbringing and chosen for his hero the notorious gunman Billy the Kid. It had taken the combined forces of constant prayer and a stiff dose of reality to bring him to his senses and set him back on the right path. What if no one had been praying for him or taken the time to try to set him straight?

The thought sobered him. The Wingates needed God in their lives, and in order to comprehend His love for them, they needed to see it exemplified in the lives of those who knew Him. Violet was doing a fine job of that already, Willie thought with a pang of guilt. His behavior, on the other hand, would have to undergo some major changes in order to reflect any semblance of Christlikeness.

At least they'd made some progress tonight. What a question to be asked right out of the blue! Apparently, Jessie's illness had a more sobering effect on them than he'd thought. It would have been nice if they'd followed through tonight, but he could take heart in knowing he'd presented the gospel clearly enough that they could understand. At least that seed had been planted.

He ought to tell Violet. She'd be thrilled to hear of their interest, and she could pray with him that all three of the young Wingates would come to trust Jesus as their Savior in the near future. The thought buoyed him and he headed to the kitchen.

❧

He found a mountain of unwashed dishes, but no Violet. Come to think of it, he hadn't heard her once since bringing the boys into the house. Thoroughly concerned, he hurried down the hallway to Jessie's room, his boots ringing on the wooden floor with each long stride.

He halted three feet short of the door to Jessie's bedroom. Their agreement during the quarantine had been to keep himself and the boys completely away from the sick child. He and Violet hadn't even been in the same room since the morning Jessie got sick. Now he hesitated, not wanting to take a chance on spreading the disease to Jessie's brothers, but feeling deep inside himself that something must be wrong.

Even though he and Violet kept their distance, he could always discern her presence. He couldn't remember being in the house the past few days without hearing the low murmur of her voice comforting Jessie or her light footsteps while she hurried from one household chore to another. This sudden silence unnerved him.

He crept closer to the doorway. Light from the kerosene lamp spilled out into the hallway, painting a bright rectangle at his feet. Willie steeled himself for whatever he might find and peered into the room.

Jessie lay deep in slumber on the bed, her hair spreading around her pale face in a golden pool. The gentle rise and fall of her chest assured Willie she slept peacefully. His gaze moved to the chair next to the bed. Violet slumped back against the cushion, eyes closed and head sagging. The cloth she used to wipe Jessie's brow dangled from one limp hand.

Willie's throat constricted. Had Violet succumbed to the disease as well? He started to enter the room, then stopped and observed her more closely from where he stood. Her color seemed good, he noted with relief, except for those dark smudges under her eyes. Probably the result of all those sleepless nights sitting up with Jessie. He watched her breathing. Good, smooth and even. From all appearances, she merely slept the sleep of utter exhaustion, and who could blame her?

He hesitated in the doorway, wondering if he should wake Violet. She would be mortified to think she had dozed off while tending to her charge. No, he decided, let her sleep. She needed all the rest she could get, from the looks of her.

Willie studied her face, fascinated by the way her dark lashes fanned out over her cheeks. With those loose strands of hair floating about her face, she almost looked like a little girl herself. Better not tell her that, he thought with a chuckle.

A wave of tenderness engulfed him. How could such a frail-looking creature accomplish so much? He felt an overpowering desire to shelter Violet, to protect her from life's storms. She'd had no reason to pour out her love to three children she didn't know, except for the kindness of her heart; but she took on the responsibility without a moment's hesitation. She bore no legal obligation for them, yet here she sat, selflessly attending a little girl she met only recently, risking her own health to do so.

Hardly the actions of a woman after easy money. The thought sent a pang of contrition straight through him. Why had he taken Mary Rose and her suggestion seriously for even a moment? He had to admit the woman had charm and looks, along with ways that made a man feel special. But with all her frills and fripperies, he knew beyond a doubt that Mary Rose Downey didn't possess one-tenth of Violet's character.

The desire to ask Violet to join her prayers for Toby and Frederick to his had entered his mind the moment he'd finished his talk with the boys. Had she been awake when he found her, he knew without question she would have welcomed the opportunity. Violet didn't flaunt her faith; she lived it out in every aspect of her life. He'd been aware of it without noticing it since the beginning. Now that he took the time to think things through, he wondered at not picking up on such an obvious character trait more quickly.

He sent one last lingering glance her way, then withdrew back down the hallway and let himself out the front door, treading lightly so as not to waken the sleeping occupants. His footsteps made little sound on the hard-packed path between the house and his cabin. A hundred thoughts clamored for attention, most having to do with the change he'd experienced that evening. What had happened in that brief span of time to make him look at the Wingate children and Violet in an entirely new way?

Only You, Lord. Only You. He lay on his back and pondered, marveling at the ways God had shown Himself to be at work in his life. The boys' subdued attitudes evidenced a depth of concern for their sister he hadn't suspected before now. And then those questions they'd peppered him with!

Willie chuckled softly. He sure hadn't seen them coming. Had he given the boys the information they needed to fully understand Christ's sacrifice? Explaining the most important decision life held wasn't something he did on a regular basis, but his parents and pastor had always made it clear that being equipped to do so was the responsibility of every believer, not just the clergy.

He thought back over the answers he'd given, then nodded. Both Frederick and Toby seemed to understand the concept of sin and their need to be saved from its penalty.

Willie snuggled his blanket closer under his chin and fell asleep whispering a prayer for the salvation of both the boys and their sister.

eleven

"Hello there!"

Willie looked up from the woodpile to see a man and woman standing next to the gatepost where the quarantine sign glinted in the noontime sun. Must be neighbors he hadn't met yet. He waved to acknowledge the greeting and sauntered over to exchange a few words, pleased at the prospect of seeing new faces. Aside from Doc's visits and the occasional howdy Jeb McCurdy hollered from the road, he hadn't talked to anyone but Violet and the kids since the quarantine began.

He stopped at the prescribed distance from the newcomers and dipped his head in greeting. The couple stared back at him without speaking, then the man turned and jabbed a finger at the quarantine notice.

"What's the meaning of this?" he barked.

Willie felt the hackles rise on the back of his neck. He hadn't been in the area long, but he'd met enough locals to know he could expect friendly treatment from most of them. Apparently this fellow didn't belong to the majority.

"Just what it says," he responded, not bothering to temper the frosty tone in his voice. "There's scarlet fever here. We're under quarantine."

The woman's clear brown eyes widened. She gasped and clapped a hand to her throat. "Violet?" she faltered.

Willie relaxed a fraction. At least she seemed to care somewhat about the farm's occupants. "No, Ma'am," he replied. "It's Jessie, the little girl who's staying here." Instead of the relief he expected to see, the woman's expression grew more confused.

Her companion glowered. "What little girl?" he demanded. "And who on earth are you?"

Willie bristled at the peremptory tone. "Name's Willie

93

Bradley." He drew himself erect and took on a combative stance. "Of the Double B Ranch in northern New Mexico Territory. And you are. . .?"

The man's face darkened like a thundercloud. He planted both fists on his hips and scowled. "I'm Daniel Moore, and this is my wife, Rachel. We live here."

🍃

Once, Willie had watched a cowboy stun a wild-eyed steer by delivering a well-aimed blow between its eyes with a two-by-four. Now he knew just how that steer must have felt. He drew his lower jaw up from its sagging position and tried to gather his whirling thoughts into some semblance of order.

Rachel and Daniel. Of course. He'd heard Violet mention them often enough. He'd even seen a photograph of the two of them on the mantel. Why hadn't he made the connection himself?

What brought them back from their trip so soon? Mentally, he calculated the date and groaned inwardly. Their return wasn't early at all. With all the upheaval surrounding Jessie's illness, he'd lost track of time. *Violet must have too, or she would have mentioned something about expecting them any day.*

He had to quit standing there like a dunce. Willie struggled to find something suitable to say. "Welcome home. How was your trip?"

Judging from Rachel and Daniel's startled expressions, his overture hadn't had the desired effect. Daniel's sandy brows drew together in a straight line, and he took a step forward. Rachel grasped his arm. "Let's hear what he has to say," she counseled.

Daniel halted in midstride and crossed his arms. "All right." He threw Willie a challenging glance. "Let's hear it. I want to know who you are and why you're here and why I shouldn't horsewhip you off this property."

Much as he wanted to turn tail and run, Willie forced himself to stand his ground. Up to now, given the isolation of the farm, he hadn't paid much thought to how their situation might look to outside eyes. And he'd never considered how this scene might appear to Violet's relatives. He knew his behavior had been above reproach; so did Violet. But how would her sister and brother-in-law take his being there with Violet, alone except for three children who were strangers to them? A hard knot of worry formed in his stomach.

"It's kind of a long story," he began, feeling his way along like a man crossing a raging stream. "I brought three orphaned kids out here to meet their guardian, but I've had trouble locating him. Your sister met them and wanted to take them in until he'd been found. The sheriff thought that was a good idea too, so the kids have been staying in the house with Violet and I've been sleeping in the cabin out back."

He took note of Daniel's grim expression. He hadn't relaxed, but he hadn't come through the gate either. That might be a promising sign. "The little girl—Jessie—came down with scarlet fever, and Doc Hathaway put up the quarantine sign. We've tried to keep the boys away from her, and so far they haven't caught it. If all goes well, the quarantine should be lifted before too long."

Daniel glared at him through slitted eyes. "You're telling me you've been staying out here, unchaperoned, for all that time? And you expect me not to shoot you?"

Willie tried to moisten his lips, but his mouth had gone bone dry. He had an idea how his father might have felt had Lizzie been in a similar situation. Squaring his shoulders, he returned Daniel's unblinking stare as steadily as he could. "That's what I'm saying, all right. It's not a normal situation, I'll grant you that. But I can tell you, and I'm sure Violet will too, that nothing untoward has happened. . .and nothing will."

He maintained his position, willing himself not to look away, even when he heard the creak of approaching buggy wheels. A raspy voice broke the tense silence.

"Well, look who's back. You catching the folks up on what all's happened lately, Willie?"

Willie darted a glance sideways and caught a glimpse of

Jeb McCurdy's face, aglow with neighborly benevolence. "Something like that." He shifted his gaze back to Daniel's stony countenance.

"It's a good thing Willie was around when all this happened," Jeb went on, not seeming to catch the underlying tension of the moment. "If Miss Violet hadn't had his help, she'd have been plumb snowed under, trying to take care of all those young'uns on her own."

The knot in Willie's stomach loosened a fraction. Thank goodness for Jeb's timing. He couldn't have asked for a more fortuitous circumstance than to have his behavior vouched for by a trusted neighbor.

"You seem to be forgetting one thing, Jeb," Daniel replied in a dry tone. "If he and his crew hadn't been around, none of this would have happened, would it?"

Jeb scratched his grizzled chin and shot an unerring stream of tobacco juice toward a manzanita bush. "I s'pose you may have a point there," he muttered. Then he brightened. "Be that as it may, I can't recall ever seeing Miss Violet so full of life as she's been since those younguns showed up. Tended to 'em like a mother hen, she has, and happy as can be to do it. A body could see that right off.

"As for this young feller here," he continued, "he's been every inch the gentleman, doing everything he could to help ease the burden. Why, he even hustled into town to fetch Doc Hathaway when the little girl took sick. Got him out here in record time, he did. And he wasn't even on the premises when Doc posted the quarantine notice; but as soon as he got back, he took it on himself to cross over and look after the boys and the chores to give Violet a free hand at taking care of that little one. I got that from Doc hisself," he added with an emphatic nod. "He was plumb impressed by that, and I guess you should be too."

He nodded to punctuate his lengthy speech, gathered up the reins, and clucked to his horse. Willie watched his progress down the road for a moment, struck by the fortuitous arrival of his unexpected champion. A spark of hope flickered. Surely Daniel and Rachel couldn't help but be moved by McCurdy's impassioned defense. He cast a hopeful look in their direction.

Daniel eyed him thoughtfully, then looked at his wife. "Old Jeb seems quite taken with him."

Rachel, whose demeanor had gone from amazed to suspicious during McCurdy's recitation, exchanged glances with her husband, then lifted her chin in a way that reminded Willie of Violet and looked directly at him. "Just for your information, Mr. Bradley, a recommendation from Jeb McCurdy doesn't go a long way toward setting my mind at ease. Don't think we're going to accept this situation just on his say-so. I'd like to speak to my sister."

Willie swallowed again. The knot seemed to move from his stomach to his throat. He tried to force the words past the obstruction. "She's resting right now, and I hate to disturb her," he said, hoping his words carried a ring of sincerity. "She's worked so hard at taking care of Jessie that she's just about worn herself out."

Rachel turned a troubled face toward Daniel. "Do you think we ought to go on in, as Mr. Bradley did?"

Her husband gave her a long, appraising look, then drew a deep breath and let it out slowly. "I don't want to leave Violet in this situation any more than you do. But I'm not willing to risk your health either. Let's look at the facts. This situation has apparently been going on practically since we left. There's nothing we can do to change that. Why don't we go into town and check things out with Doc and see what he says? I'd feel a lot better if he gives this whole thing his approval."

"Why don't you talk to Sheriff Dolan too?" put in Willie. "We've gotten to know each other fairly well, and I'm sure he'd be willing to vouch for me." The measuring look Daniel gave him told Willie his shot had hit home. Dolan held the respect of people in these parts; a good word from him would do a lot to allay their doubts.

Daniel paused as if considering, then gave a decisive nod. "That's what we'll do." He helped Rachel back into the buggy and climbed into the seat. "If they both put in a good word for you, we'll find a room in town and check in with you every day until the quarantine's over. If they don't. . .well, you'd better pray we don't hear anything to contradict that glowing recommendation you got from McCurdy." He flicked the whip and set the horse off down the road.

Willie watched the buggy recede until it disappeared in the distance. He rubbed the taut muscles in the back of his neck with one hand. He knew he had won a reprieve. How temporary that reprieve might be remained to be seen.

❧

"Well, Doc?" Violet watched the gray-haired physician put his stethoscope away and purse his lips.

He regarded Jessica with a long, surveying look, then his face broke into a pleased smile. "She's past it," he announced. "Have her take it easy for the next week or so, but for all intents and purposes, you can consider her recovered."

The air left Violet's lungs in a whoosh of gratitude. "Thank goodness! What about the boys?"

Doc bent to fasten the latch on his medical bag. "I checked them before I looked young Jessica over. They're fine. No sign of scarlet fever. . .or anything else, barring a streak of boyish orneriness." Faded blue eyes twinkled over half-moon glasses, and Doc squeezed her shoulder in a fatherly gesture. "I'm ready to lift the quarantine, Violet. You've done a fine job, just fine. You should feel proud of yourself."

All Violet felt was a profound sense of relief. She had done it. She had weathered the most difficult challenge of her life and prevailed. She tilted her head back and a laugh gurgled from her throat. No more worries about keeping the children apart. No more strain of wondering whether one of the boys would contract the disease, prolonging their separation from the rest of the world. She could sleep for a whole night in her own bed without having to keep watch on Jessie. She could. . .

"Rachel!" Violet exclaimed. "Doc, does this mean Rachel and Daniel can come home?"

"Just as soon as I take the sign down, if your sister doesn't rip it loose before I can get my hands on it." Doc chuckled. "She's been after me every time I came back into town. When I told her there was a good chance your ordeal was nearly over, she followed me out in her buggy. Want to come out with me?"

"Yes! Well. . .maybe not just yet." Violet's gaze swept around the room, taking in the unsightly disarray. More clutter awaited her in the kitchen, and goodness only knew what chaos lurked in other parts of the house. She fixed Doc with a pleading gaze. "Do you think you could take your time getting out there? Give me just a few more minutes?"

His eyes widened. "After all this time, you want to stretch it out even longer?" He watched her scurry around the room to snatch up dishes and soiled clothes with frantic haste and smiled. "I'll see what I can do, but I won't promise much. Your sister's just as eager to get inside as you are to stall her." He strode down the hallway at an easy pace, his rumbling laughter audible until the closing of the front door cut it off.

Violet hefted her armload and headed for the kitchen. A quick glance as she passed the living room door confirmed her worst fears. Seeing to Jessie's needs during her illness and making sure no one else came down with scarlet fever had been preeminent. Now that Doc had declared the crisis over, routine chores reared their heads again, needing her attention.

What to do with the dirty clothes? She darted a glance around the kitchen and stuffed them into a cupboard, then turned to grab the broom. If she could just—

"Violet!" The glad cry from the doorway stopped her in her tracks. She pivoted and ran to embrace her sister.

"Oh, Rachel, it's so good to have you home! I've missed you." She would have continued to hold her sister close, savoring the comfort of her presence, but Rachel pulled away and stepped back to study her at arm's length.

Worry lines appeared in Rachel's forehead. "Violet Canfield, what on earth has been going on here? You look like you've been dragged behind a team of runaway horses."

Violet raked her fingers through her hair, encountering a mass of snarls and tangles. Maybe her first move should have been to spend time in front of her mirror preparing for their reunion. "We've had quite a time, I'll admit that. But things are going to get back to normal again right away, you'll see. It's been a little hectic with Jessie sick and all. I'm just happy the boys didn't catch it too."

"Ah, yes. Let's talk about this little family you've acquired while we've been gone. What happened? We leave you alone one time and come back to find four strangers have taken up residence and there's a quarantine notice on our gate." Rachel raised an eyebrow and planted both hands on her hips in a gesture Violet recognized from innumerable encounters in the past.

She lifted her chin in a gesture she hoped would hide its trembling from Rachel's keen gaze. "It's no great mystery. The children needed help; I helped them. It's as simple as that."

Rachel rolled her eyes and huffed. "Simple? Violet, there has to be more to it than that. What kind of help did they need, and why did they need it from you? Why couldn't Mr. Bradley help them?"

"Oh." She turned and traced her finger across the windowsill. "Well, it seems rather silly now, but at the beginning they were looking for protection *from* Wil—Mr. Bradley." She squeezed her eyes shut and waited for the explosion.

She didn't wait long.

"And so you just told them to come in and live with you—then invited this man they were afraid of to stay here too, is that it? Honestly, Violet, don't you ever think? He could have been some kind of criminal, or worse! And here you are by yourself, opening the place up to total strangers and not mentioning a word of it in your letters."

"Sheriff Dolan came out here with him," Violet muttered,

keeping her face averted. "He thought it was okay for them all to stay."

Rachel gripped Violet by the shoulders and turned her around. Anxiety darkened her eyes and her taut facial features showed the depth of her concern. "Honey, you have to understand that this is not the same as bringing home a baby squirrel or a bird with a broken wing. There's more responsibility involved in taking care of children. A lot more."

Violet swept away Rachel's hands and put the width of the kitchen between them. "Don't you think I know that by now? I've done nothing but tend to their needs since they got here. I've cooked and cleaned and mended and washed. I've read stories and played games and settled squabbles and tucked them into bed at night. Since Jessie's been sick, I've spent nearly every moment keeping her fever down and racking my brain to try to find something to tempt her appetite. Don't try to tell me how much responsibility's involved," she cried, her voice breaking. "I know good and well just how hard it is to take care of a child!"

The pent-up emotions of the recent ordeal broke through the dam she'd erected, and the tears poured forth. Violet wrapped her arms around herself and bent double, racked with sobs. Through the turbulent storm, she was vaguely aware of Rachel's arms supporting her, then settling her in a chair. She savored the luxury of leaning into her sister's embrace and listening to her comforting voice.

"I'm sorry, Violet," Rachel crooned. "I didn't mean to hurt you. I've been so worried ever since we got back, and I guess it just all spilled out." She stroked Violet's hair back from her forehead. "Go ahead and cry it out, Honey. You've been through a lot."

Violet tried to speak, but sobs still shook her body. Over the sound of her own weeping she heard Daniel's voice: "She's not getting sick, is she?"

"I don't think so," Rachel replied. "She's just tired and overworked, and I lit into her without thinking."

Violet could tell by the creaking of the floor that Daniel had moved to a position near the living room doorway. "I've been talking to the Bradley fellow," he said. "Seems like a decent enough sort. From what he tells me, Violet's done an amazing job looking after the kids. To tell you the truth," he said, lowering his voice, "I never thought she had it in her. We ought to be real proud."

"I am." Rachel dropped her voice to a whisper and held Violet close while the tempest subsided. "Look at her, Daniel. This isn't the dreamy-eyed little sister we left behind just a few weeks ago."

"It isn't the same house we left behind either." Daniel's chuckle removed any sting from his words.

"I know. But with some extra hands helping, it won't take long to get it back in shape."

The warmth of her sister's caring offer lifted the burden of guilt from Violet's shoulders. She drew a shaky breath and mopped at her face with her sleeve. Daniel pressed a handkerchief into her hand, and she gave him a wobbly smile.

"Welcome home," she told him in a voice that trembled only a little.

"It's good to be back." He smiled down at her, his deep green eyes gleaming with humor. "Even if it isn't quite the welcome we'd expected. It sounds like you've had a time of it."

"It's been a challenge," she conceded, giving her cheeks a final swipe and getting to her feet. "But we managed."

"So I hear." Daniel folded his arms and regarded her thoughtfully. "You certainly have a champion in Willie Bradley. He couldn't say enough good things about the way you took on the kids and kept things running."

"Did he?" Violet felt the blood rush to her cheeks and used the handkerchief to fan herself. Goodness, she wasn't coming down with a fever after all, was she?

Rachel's brows drew together in a quick frown. "But I thought the two of you weren't on good terms, with you feeling you had to protect the children and all."

The heat rose in Violet's face. She didn't exactly feel sick, but maybe she'd better get a cool drink and lie down for a while, just to make sure. "That was just at the beginning," she reassured her sister. "The children felt he didn't like them, and I'll admit I thought the same thing at first. But he's been wonderful to them lately. . .to all of us," she added softly.

Rachel raised her brows and looked at Daniel. "And where is this remarkable man? I'd like to get a chance to speak with him under better circumstances."

"He headed into town as soon as we finished talking," Daniel replied. "Said he needed to make up for lost time and get back to looking for Thurman Hadlock, although a less likely prospect for raising children is hard to imagine. At any rate, now that he's free to check around again, it surely won't be too much longer before he can turn the kids over to him and get on back to his ranch."

Violet blinked. "I guess he'll be happy to be leaving," she said. The Wingates and Willie had become such a regular part of her life of late, she hadn't thought much about the fact that they wouldn't be staying on permanently. She changed her mind about having a fever. The warm glow departed in a rush, to be replaced by a cold, leaden feeling she couldn't explain.

twelve

"Hadlock? Sure, I know him." The whiskered miner leaned against the wall of the mercantile and scratched his chest through holes in a shirt that looked like it hadn't been washed in months.

Willie moved upwind. *Somehow, that doesn't surprise me. He looks just like the type of person I'd picture Hadlock with.* Odd how Hadlock had taken on such a clear image in his mind after listening to Violet's perceptions of the man. She had influenced him more than he'd realized. "Can you tell me where to find him?"

His grubby companion shrugged and cocked his head. "How far you willin' to travel?" He cackled at Willie's bewildered expression. "He took off for San Francisco over a month ago. Just one more of his harebrained schemes for gettin' rich, I reckon, but he was plumb fired up about it."

Willie tried not to show how much this news rocked him. "Any idea when he'll be back?"

"Hard to tell. I would have expected him back before this, but if he got sidetracked by some blond gold digger, who's to say? It oughtn't be more than another week or two, though. If he did make any money, he'll run through it all by then. If I see him, you want me to tell him anything for you?"

Willie considered the man's probable trustworthiness at conveying a message. "No, thanks. I'll wait and talk to him myself." He strode back along Montezuma Street, trying to keep an impassive expression while he assessed this new information.

A week or two to wait! And here he'd already spent three weeks chasing his tail trying to find the man, when all along he hadn't even been in the territory. Willie slammed his fist

104

into the rough wood of the market and received a reproving glance from a passing matron. He continued on his way, fighting to keep his frustration under control.

He thought back. When had Monroe come to the Double B? And how long before that had he sent word to Hadlock to expect his arrival with the Wingates? Willie made a quick mental calculation and groaned aloud, earning him another uneasy look from a passerby. In all likelihood, Hadlock hadn't even received Monroe's message before heading for parts west. In that case, he had no idea he would be welcoming the children of his late friend into his home upon his return.

Could things possibly get any worse? It hadn't even been his idea to make this trip in the first place, he reminded himself on the way back to the farm. He never volunteered to ride herd on a group of kids who made a pack of wolves look tame in comparison. He shuddered, remembering how they'd run him ragged on the way out, caused him to miss their train, then left him stranded out in the middle of nowhere.

If that hadn't been enough, they'd made him out to be some kind of wild-eyed monster. And people had believed it of him. Gloomy memories of their trip came back to haunt him, memories that even the boys' improved behavior of late couldn't displace.

What on earth was he going to do now? Another week of trying to cope with those three would be enough to send him around the bend. And where would he go? Did he dare ask if he and the kids could stay on at the farm? There had to be a way. He simply couldn't handle them all on his own.

Slow down. Take it easy. God's in control. It took every bit of his willpower to remind himself of this fact on the trip back to the farm. Gradually, the truth of God's sovereignty seeped into his mind and calmed his soul. A week wasn't forever. Even two weeks didn't compare with eternity. He could hold out that long.

By then, surely Hadlock would have returned. And if not, Monroe should be able to travel soon. He could come out and take the kids off Willie's hands, reclaiming the responsibility that had been his to begin with. Cheered by this thought, Willie turned his mind to how he might persuade Daniel to let his little band stay on.

&

"Let me get this straight." Daniel climbed down from the loft and slapped the hay dust off his clothes. "You want to stay around and work for me to earn your keep and the kids'?"

"That's about the size of it." Willie coiled and uncoiled his lariat to give his jittery hands something to do. He tried in vain to read Daniel's expression and gauge the other man's probable reaction to the proposal he'd just made.

Daniel gave Willie a long, measuring look, then grinned and stuck out his hand. "Sounds good to me. I could use some help with the planting, and it'll be a way to keep the kids around here a while longer. I have a feeling we'd have a hard time prying them loose from Violet," he said with a chuckle. "She's grown mighty attached to them. So have Rachel and I, for that matter. It'll be hard to see them go when the time comes."

Willie returned his firm handclasp with a silent prayer of gratitude and tried not to show his astonishment at this news. How anyone as levelheaded as Daniel Moore could cotton to those kids was beyond him, but he didn't have any intention of jeopardizing his position by enlightening the man as to their true natures. He could only pray they'd maintain their current level of behavior until after they left the farm.

"I appreciate it," he told Daniel. "And I'll be sure to make good on my part of the deal."

Daniel nodded agreement with a readiness that took Willie by surprise. "I know you will. Out here, you learn to size up a man pretty quickly. Truth to tell, I have a feeling I'll come out ahead in this bargain. Why don't you start out by fixing that fence at the south end of the pasture?" He pointed out the tools Willie would need and a pile of posts and left.

Willie watched him walk away, then began loading the fencing material into the back of the wagon with a thrill of gratification. For the first time in his life, he'd been judged on his own merit and found worthy of approval; it was enough to make a man walk mighty tall.

❧

A gentle breeze teased the young spring grass coming up in the pasture. Toby romped across the yard, kicking up his heels like a young colt. On the porch, Frederick pondered his next move on the checkerboard set up on a low table between his chair and Jessica's, while Violet fussed over the little girl, making sure she was safely bundled up against the evening air.

Daniel watched from his seat in one of the matching rocking chairs and shook his head. "It's plenty warm out here, Violet," he said with a tolerant smile. "She's not going to take a chill."

Violet finished tucking a light shawl around Jessie, then gave a self-deprecating laugh. "You're right; I'm hovering over her like a mother hen. I just want to make sure. That was quite a scare we had with her." She tenderly stroked Jessie's head and took a seat on the other side of Rachel, who rummaged through her mending basket. She picked up a piece of embroidery and began stitching.

Willie watched the homey scene from his seat on the porch steps, savoring the memory of the roast chicken dinner he'd enjoyed a short time before. He laced his fingers around one knee and stretched the other leg out with a sigh of satisfaction. Kids playing while the adults sat around the porch sharing an easy camaraderie—the scene could have been taken straight from his own family.

He closed his eyes and drew a long, slow breath, enjoying the smell of fresh-turned earth. How long had it been since he'd felt so content? Well before the advent of the Wingate clan in his life, he thought with a wry chuckle. Life hadn't seemed this idyllic for a long time.

With every day that passed, Willie felt increasingly comfortable around Daniel. The man had his unqualified respect. The more time he spent with Daniel, the more he found him to be hard-working, expecting much from himself and those around him; but he balanced that expectation with an innate sense of fairness. Much of what he saw in Daniel reminded him of the traits he admired in his father and uncle, including his deep faith.

Daniel's relationship with Rachel reminded him of his parents' too. Their obvious love for each other was the same kind he longed for in his own marriage someday. And after the awkwardness of their first meeting, both of them had gone out of their way to make him feel like he fit right into the family circle as an accepted part of the group. No wonder it didn't take any effort to feel right at home.

"What's this, Miss Violet?" Toby ran up the porch steps. His pounding boots narrowly avoided contact with Willie's shin. "I found it over by the well." He held up a delicate yellow flower trailing long spurs for her inspection.

Violet lifted the drooping blossom with the tip of her finger. "Do you remember its name?" She gave him an encouraging smile. "We talked about it the other day."

Toby frowned and studied his specimen with the tip of his tongue protruding from one corner of his mouth. "Clummine?" He looked up at Violet for confirmation.

"That's close. It's a columbine."

"Col-um-bine." Toby pronounced each syllable with care.

"Good for you!" Violet gave him a squeeze. "Can you find some other flowers we've studied? Look around; there are lots of them just starting to bloom."

Willie moved his legs out of Toby's way, and the little boy scampered away from the house in search of more specimens. Jessie watched him with a wistful expression that tugged at Willie's heart.

"Can I look for flowers too?" she pleaded.

Violet looked askance at the request, then appeared to reconsider. "Poor Jessie. You haven't gotten to play outdoors for ages, have you? All right, but no running. You can still find plenty of flowers to pick if you just walk between here and the edge of the field."

"I promise." Jessie's smile fairly shone. "Cross my heart." She stepped past Willie and bent her head to study the ground, with Frederick at her heels. A moment later, she squealed in delight and stooped to pluck a tiny bloom hidden in the grass.

Willie watched them, a warm glow spreading through him at their childish enjoyment. Maybe all these kids had needed all along was a little love and attention. Violet provided plenty of that, all right. Hard to imagine how such a delicate frame could hold so much affection, but she had all they needed and plenty to spare.

"You just made Jessie one happy little girl," he told her, meeting her gaze straight on. Her smile shone as radiantly as Jessie's had.

"I almost didn't let her go," she admitted. "But then she gave me that look. . . ." She shook her head and laughed. "How could anyone argue with those incredible eyes?"

Willie knew exactly what she meant. Just looking into Violet's blue eyes made him feel like he was falling into a deep forest pool. If a man didn't watch his step, he could be in over his head before he knew it.

The scrape of Rachel's rocker on the wooden porch floor brought him back to the moment. Willie blinked and tried to assume a nonchalant air. He didn't know just where that errant thought had come from, and he sure didn't want anyone else to suspect the direction his mind had just taken. He had enough problems on his hands without making the Moores worry about his intentions.

He shot a quick glance at Daniel and felt his neck grow warm under the older man's scrutiny. Daniel's face held a knowing smirk that told Willie his calf-eyed stare hadn't gone unnoticed. Toby ran up on the porch again, his arrival providing a welcome distraction.

"Look at this one. Isn't it pretty?" He held aloft a pinkish flower that reminded Willie of his mother's snapdragons.

"I've got some too," Jessie called. She and Frederick

climbed onto the porch behind their brother, each clutching a handful of blooms for Violet's perusal.

Rachel chuckled. "It looks like you have your work cut out for you this evening. It's a good thing you're the flower expert in the family."

"Mama was a good teacher," Violet replied and turned her attention to the samples before her. "Oh, my. Look at these beautiful things." She took her time examining each specimen. Toby danced from one foot to the other, awaiting her verdict. "This," she announced, twirling the slender stalk of Jessie's offering between her fingers, "is blue flax." She placed it back in Jessie's hands, and the little girl stared at it in wonder.

"Look at mine next." Frederick pointed at the clump of small white flowers in Violet's hand. "Mine have lots more petals than the others do."

"They do, don't they?" Violet held up the tiny blossoms so all the children could see them. "That's one way of identifying it. This one is a baby aster."

"There's a whole bunch of them over near the corral," Frederick volunteered. "Want me to pick more for you?"

"Why don't we let them grow right where they are?" Violet's eyes sparkled with amusement at the boy's enthusiasm. "That way, we'll be able to keep on enjoying them."

"What about mine?" Toby demanded. "What's its name?"

Violet grinned. "It's called penstemon," she told him, enunciating the word with care.

Frederick snickered at the odd name, and Toby glared at him. "It's still a pretty flower," he muttered, then descended the steps again. "I'm gonna go find another one that has a pretty name to go with it." He trotted over near the barn and gave a cry of triumph. "Look at this great big white one!" He reached for it with both hands.

"Don't touch it!" Willie hollered. "That's—" His words were cut off by a yowl from Toby. "Prickly poppy," he finished. He loped across the yard with Violet right behind him and scooped the little boy into his arms. "Are you okay? Let me see those fingers." He studied them, noting that the skin hadn't been broken. "You'll be fine, just a little sore for awhile," he told him. He set the youngster back on the ground and watched him run back to recount his injury for the others, then turned to Violet. "No real damage, but he won't be grabbing for those flowers again anytime soon."

She nodded in sympathy. "It seems like it takes a painful lesson to get through to us sometimes." She tilted her head up to look at him. "I didn't know you were acquainted with flower names."

Willie laughed. "I'm not. I just happened to recognize that one from an encounter I had with the stuff when I was about Toby's age. It was one of those painful lessons, all right." He grinned at Violet and their gazes locked. There was that sensation of diving into dangerous water again. He could feel himself plunging down farther into its depths with every passing moment. He didn't know if he'd ever reach the surface again and wasn't sure he wanted to.

Violet, too, seemed to recognize their special connection. He could see the pulse flutter at the base of her throat, and she probed him with a questioning gaze. She laid her hand on his arm.

Her fingers sent shafts of fire right through the fabric of his shirt. Willie flinched as though stung and regretted the involuntary reaction when Violet snatched her hand away and clasped it against her stomach. Neither of them spoke, but a message seemed to pass between them just the same.

thirteen

Willie hung up the heavy harness and went into his cabin full of satisfaction at the amount of plowing he'd done. He poured water into the basin on the tiny table beside his bed and sluiced it over his face and hands. Sputtering, he reached for the towel hanging on a nail in front of him and shivered. The weather might be getting warmer by the day, but that water felt downright cold.

He combed his hair and checked his appearance in the cracked mirror he'd fastened to the wall. He smoothed a stray lock of wavy hair back off his forehead and decided his appearance would pass muster. After a day spent hauling sacks of seed, Daniel wouldn't look much more energetic than he did. He just hoped his inner feelings wouldn't show on his face.

Not even to himself did he want to admit how his pulse quickened around Violet these days. He sure didn't want Rachel or Daniel to have any inkling of the turmoil he felt when Violet was anywhere near him, not after they had extended their hospitality by letting him and the Wingate kids stay with them. And they wouldn't, if he could help it.

He tried not to think about Violet's response, or her lack of it. She hadn't said a word since their conversation near the barn, and he wasn't about to bring it up.

Willie tucked his shirttail in and took a deep breath, then headed up the familiar path to the house, determined to act as though he felt no different tonight than any other. He gave a perfunctory tap on the kitchen door and walked inside, ready to dole out a light compliment about the savory aroma coming from the oven. His words of praise died on his lips when he

112

saw the white-faced group seated at the table.

A quick glance told him only the three other adults were in the room and a sick feeling of dread wrenched at his stomach. "What's wrong? Is it one of the kids?"

Rachel gazed at him wordlessly and shook her head. Violet merely stared down at her hands, clasped together in a white-knuckled grip on the tablecloth. Finally, Daniel broke the uneasy silence.

"You'd better hear what's going around town. I don't know any other way to tell you than just to say it straight out." He pressed his lips together and cleared his throat, then went on. "There's talk circulating, Willie, and it's bad. Real bad."

Willie looked from face to face, but still couldn't find a clue. "What kind of talk?"

"About you. . .and Violet. Seems there's quite a bit of speculation as to your real reason for staying out here during the quarantine." Daniel regarded him steadily.

If not for the steady ticking of the mantel clock, Willie would have believed that time had frozen. Even his heart seemed to have quit beating. He stared at the people who had given him their trust and taken him in. Did he detect a difference in Daniel's and Rachel's attitude toward him? "I swear to you—" he began.

Daniel held up his hand. "I believe you. We both do. We know Violet and we've come to know you. No one can convince me anything happened out here that shouldn't have, but the story is flying around, just the same. I left half my load of seed on Samson's loading dock and came home as soon as I heard."

"Who started it?" Anger surged through Willie with an intensity that shocked him. He'd been in plenty of scraps in his younger years, but never before had he wanted so badly to strangle someone. He clenched his fists and wished he could use them on whoever said such a thing. "Give me a name and I'll put an end to it before another day is over."

Daniel held up a restraining hand. "I asked the same question. It's like trying to track down a wisp of smoke. No telling how it got started. . .or how it'll end. We'll just have to ride it out, I guess."

Willie's stomach churned with suppressed rage. He grasped the door handle.

Rachel reached out a hand. "Aren't you going to eat?"

"I'm not hungry." With that blunt statement, Willie stepped out into the fresh spring evening. He stood on the porch a moment, listening. Crickets chirped; blades of new grass whispered together in the soft breeze. To all outward appearances, life went on just as it always had. But Willie felt the difference deep within him, a burning fury that demanded satisfaction. With angry strides, he started toward his cabin.

"Willie."

He registered the quiet voice even through the pounding of blood in his temples. He stopped, turned, and walked slowly back to the porch where Violet stood in the glow of light from the kitchen window. He took a step nearer. Even in the dimness, he could discern her pallor.

His heart melted and guilt threatened to gnaw a hole straight through him. Violet had only reached out to minister to some needy orphans and their testy keeper. She didn't deserve this kind of ugly talk or the pain it caused. Why on earth hadn't he had the sense to foresee something like this happening? He knew the answer, and it galled him. He'd been so focused on his own troubles that he never considered what staying there might cost her. At the moment, he didn't know who he wanted to vent his anger on more—the purveyor of the rumor or himself.

"Willie," she said again. The pale golden light shimmered on her hair. He wished he could see those amazing blue eyes of hers, but they remained in shadow.

"I won't let whoever's responsible get away with this."

"It's going to be all right."

"All right?" The words tore out of him. How could anything be all right again?

She nodded, sorrow and resignation evident in her movement. "Let it go. There's nothing you can do."

Wasn't there? As soon as he figured out who'd set such vicious slander in motion, he'd be only too happy to throttle him.

"There's no point in trying to track this down," she continued, as if she'd read his mind. "A rumor is like a pillow that bursts and sends feathers floating everywhere. You can mend the rip, but all those feathers will keep on floating around, especially if you keep stirring them up even more. It's best just to let them all settle down of their own accord. They will eventually, you know."

"But in the meantime—"

"There's no truth to the story, is there?"

Willie jerked his head back. "You know there isn't!"

"Of course I do. We both know the truth, and that's what we have to hang on to. People will either believe the story or they won't; there's nothing you or I can do to change that. All we can do is hold our heads high and walk tall through this. God is our witness, and He knows we have nothing to be ashamed of."

True enough, but it didn't help assuage his sense of justice. "I'm sorry I got you into this."

Violet turned her head slightly, and her lips parted in a tiny smile. "It seems to me this started out as my idea. As I recall, you had rather strong feelings against it in the beginning."

Willie grinned in spite of himself at the memory of their earliest encounter. "All the same, I'd still like to find the fellow who started all this."

"I understand, Willie, believe me. I've felt the same way ever since Daniel came home with the news. But adding wrong to wrong won't make it any better. We'll just have to weather this and remember that God is in control."

Her gentle voice held a confidence that echoed in Willie's mind through the long hours of that sleepless night. He'd known that Violet Canfield had an abiding faith, but he never suspected its depth before now. It put his own reaction to shame.

Back home he'd chafed at the feeling that no one took him seriously, but that didn't begin to compare to the gravity of his present position. Being considered a well-meaning, if incompetent, kid bore no resemblance to being labeled a philanderer.

And he'd dragged Violet down with him. The knowledge only added to the bitterness of his despair.

One thing he knew: He had to shed the kids as quickly as possible. He needed to get out of there so he wouldn't do anything else to bring more pain to Violet.

≥≈

Just after first light, Willie took the wagon and headed into town to pick up the rest of Daniel's seed. He pulled the horses to a halt in front of Samson's Market and took his time setting the brake and climbing down from the seat.

He scanned the people passing by, trying to discern any telltale glances that might be cast his way. Did anyone look at him differently this morning than they had a week ago? Several men nodded when they walked past him, and he couldn't decide whether their smiles were genuine or held a note of sly amusement.

Hard to tell. With his feelings so much on edge, it would be all too easy to see scorn where none existed. Not only that, but he had no idea how long this story had been circulating. The attitudes he had accepted as normal might have been covering disdain for weeks. The thought left a sour taste in his mouth.

He finished his business in short order, then walked to the telegraph office on the off chance Monroe had sent a wire to tell him when to expect his arrival. To his surprise, the clerk reached for a yellow slip of paper even before he gave his name. He hurried outside and found a spot away from any curious eyes.

Let it be soon. He opened the paper.

Regret to inform Lewis ill with pleurisy STOP
Will advise when able to travel to Arizona STOP
Pa

Willie read the message three times, hoping he'd somehow misunderstood its import. Each time, he came to the same conclusion: Once again, his cousin had managed to leave him stranded. His fist crumpled the telegram into a wrinkled yellow wad. It seemed the longer he stayed in Prescott, the deeper he got into a situation he never wanted to be a part of in the first place.

❧

"Cow pats, Miss Violet? Are you sure?"

Violet looked at the astonishment on the three upturned faces before her and put a hand over her mouth to cover her smile. "Quite sure," she said when she had regained her composure. "The pioneers used them for fuel on their travels west. And more often than not, it was the children's job to collect them."

Jessica's lips curled in horror. "Did they have to wait behind the cows while they. . .they. . ."

This time Violet couldn't control the laugh that burst forth. "No, Honey. There had been plenty of cows on the trail long before them. Remember we talked about how people often used oxen to pull their wagons? The pats those children picked up had been out there for some time. They were quite dry, I promise you."

Frederick raised a skeptical eyebrow. "Well, if they were dry, I suppose it wouldn't be too bad."

"No worse than the ones out there." She rose from her seat on the front porch and waved a hand to indicate the open area where their milk cow grazed in the summertime. "I've seen you kicking them when you cut across the pasture. So you see, it really wasn't so bad. They'd just go out and fill up a sheet with them and bring them in during the day so they'd have a way to start their fires at night."

Toby's face scrunched up in thought. "I guess it's nice to know it's good for something." He joined his brother and sister on their way to the pasture to take a fresh look at the previously unappreciated material.

The sound of boots thudded on the porch steps, and she turned to see Willie smiling down at her. An answering smile spread across her face without any conscious effort on her part. He'd seemed somewhat distant since that moment near the barn, even more so since learning about the rumors. Today the liveliness had returned to his eyes, and for the second time she felt that fiery tingle dart back and forth between them.

"What got you onto that topic?" he asked with a low laugh that sent a pleasant warmth all through her.

She stared up at his sun-browned face, taking in the even features and the wavy chestnut hair that glinted flashes of red in the sunlight. His composure didn't appear to have been disturbed the slightest bit. Apparently he hadn't experienced the same reaction to their proximity. "I ran out of flower names to teach them, so I decided they could learn about how this part of the country was settled. They've been playing pioneers all morning and loving every minute of it. Up to the part about the cow pats, anyway."

Willie grinned, crinkling the creases at the corners of his eyes and doing strange things to the rhythm of Violet's heartbeat. "You've worked wonders with them. They don't seem like the same kids I brought out here."

"I've said all along they were wonderful. I don't understand how you happened to get off on the wrong foot." She noted the furrow between his eyebrows and hastened to add, "But I'm glad you've worked things out with them." She felt a warm glow of pleasure when the furrow disappeared, and his smile returned before he tipped her a nod and went back to mending fence.

The smile suited him better, she decided. Much better. How glad she was that their relationship had improved so much since his arrival! It would have been a shame to have him leave with her still thinking him a cold, uncaring man.

The thought of him leaving left a cold feeling of its own deep inside her, and she tried to keep her dismay from showing on her face. She'd gotten used to having him around. *Too* used to it, she suspected. It would be harder to see him go than she'd ever have dreamed when she first met him. Back then, she would have rejoiced in his departure and done everything she could to speed him on his way. Now. . .

Saying good-bye had never been easy for her, especially not to someone she cared about. And Willie Bradley had somehow slipped into the category of a person she cared about without her even realizing it. She shook her head and blinked back the sting of tears. She would just have to be strong and make the best of it. He'd soon be going back to a life she had no part in, and she might as well get used to that fact.

❧

Willie tamped in the last of the dirt around the fence post and shook it to test his work. Good, it didn't budge. From across the field, childish voices echoed in the twilight. With the lengthening days, the kids were determined to take advantage of every bit of daylight they could. He leaned against his shovel and watched them drag what looked like an old sheet around the pasture, tossing in cow pats as they went. From the way the sheet drooped, it looked like they'd collected quite a load.

Willie grinned at their enjoyment and gathered up his tools. Quite an idea of Violet's, getting them to play pioneer. It gave them a way to run off their energy without getting into trouble, something he heartily approved. He didn't know if he'd go quite as far as Violet and call them wonderful, but he had to admit they no longer acted like the little hoodlums he'd known at first.

He yawned and stretched. He'd done his share of slapping on brands and riding countless hours in all sorts of weather. It had hardened him physically, no doubt about it, but this farmwork used a whole different set of muscles. He hoped he could stay awake long enough to pull the blankets up over him once he stretched out on his cot.

fourteen

A full night of dreamless sleep. Just what a man needed to set him back up for another day. Willie raised his head and blinked, puzzled by the weak light that filtered into the cabin. Usually sunlight aplenty made its way through the ample cracks around the door, even in the moments just after daybreak. Could it be earlier than he supposed?

From outside came the sound of Daniel rattling the latch that opened the barn door, ready to start his after-breakfast chores. Willie sprang from his cot and pulled his shirt over his head. Dim light or not, he'd managed to oversleep.

He frowned again at the door, puzzled by the lack of illumination. Maybe a heavy bank of clouds had moved in, although he wouldn't have thought it from the looks of last night's sky. Shoving his shirttail into his waistband, he yanked open the door and jumped back when an avalanche of cascading objects showered over him.

Willie coughed and waved his hand to drive away the swirling cloud of dust and tried to get his foggy mind to figure out what was going on. Something still partially blocked the light from the doorway. He pulled down the offending object and recognized it as a sheet. It looked like the same one the kids had used to carry their collection in the night before.

No. Even those kids wouldn't. . . . He glanced down at the ankle-deep pile. The bright sunshine of a perfect spring morning streamed inside, clearly illuminating an ample heap of pioneer fire fuel. Most of which was dry.

Even when his mind had to accept the evidence at his feet, Willie could do nothing but stand and stare. How had they managed it? He moved to examine the outside of the door and

121

saw where the sheet had been tacked into place along both sides and the bottom, leaving an opening in the top wide enough for loading it with their ammunition. That explained the lack of light. He must have slept even more soundly than he thought, for them to be able to make their preparations without waking him.

He prodded one of the dry pats with the toe of his boot and looked down at his shirt and pants. No point in changing until he'd swept out the cabin. He reached for the broom.

It didn't take more than ten minutes to sweep the mess back onto the sheet and redeposit it in the pasture, but that provided more than enough time for Willie's emotional temperature to soar. By the time he'd cleaned up and changed clothes, he'd reached his boiling point. He mounted the porch steps in a single stride and entered the kitchen in a state of high dudgeon.

Three expectant faces looked up from their breakfast. "Good morning, Willie," they chorused.

"Did you sleep well?" Frederick asked.

Willie fought the urge to up-end Frederick and give some serious attention to his backside. Their intent had been to make him lose his temper and look like a wild-eyed maniac in front of Violet and her family. He would not give them that satisfaction. He drew up a chair and reached for a slice of toast.

"I slept fine. How about you?"

"Well, we were up kind of late," Jessica said. She swallowed the last of her milk as though nothing significant had occurred.

"Yeah," Toby added. "We were playing pioneer." Three muffled giggles followed his announcement.

The laughter did what outright provocation couldn't. Willie stood, sending his chair over with a clatter. "Of all the underhanded—" He broke off when Violet entered the room.

She favored him with a bright smile. "Leaving already? But you haven't even had breakfast yet."

"I thought I'd just grab this and go." He scooped the toast into his hand and slathered jam on top of it. "I got a bit of a late start this morning." He picked up his chair and set it back in place, then turned to leave.

Violet waved away his explanation. "Don't feel bad. We all oversleep sooner or later."

Willie choked but refrained from answering. He stepped past the snickering Wingates and reached for the door handle. "Don't you go giving Miss Violet any trouble today," he admonished them.

"We won't," Toby said. "Cross our hearts." He turned a loving glance on Violet, who rewarded him with a quick pat on the head.

"We'll probably play pioneer some more," Jessica put in.

Violet beamed. "Isn't it wonderful how they've taken to that game? And they seem to be learning so much from it."

Willie clenched his hands, squeezing his toast into a sticky, doughy mass.

All during the rest of the day, Willie plotted ways to teach his tormentors a lesson. They had gone too far this time. He might never be able to convince Violet of their two-faced treachery, but those kids deserved a comeuppance, and it looked like he would have to be the one to do it. Thoughts of some of his own childhood pranks drifted through his mind, evoking a reminiscent smile. The three of them had no idea who they were tangling with. They had chosen to take on a master of practical jokes who had a considerable arsenal of his own at his disposal.

He pondered ways and means, discarding one idea after another. Then the memory of his tenth summer and how he'd dealt with one particularly obnoxious visitor to the ranch came to mind. He considered the possibilities. It seemed to have all the qualities he needed. Quick. Easy to set up. Simple, yet effective. Yes, that would do nicely. He propped the shovel up against a nearby tree and set off in search of a bucket.

Just a little wider. . .no, too far. There. Willie stood back and surveyed his handiwork. The chicken coop door stood slightly ajar, as though it sagged a bit on its hinges. No one would be likely to think any more of it than that, certainly not three young kids in search of eggs. He lifted his gaze and stared proudly at the bucket he had procured from the barn, now half filled with water and impeccably balanced between the door and the building.

It would only take a slight tug on the door to bring the water splashing down on the three kids. Nothing that would hurt them, just enough to let them know they'd met their match and had better watch their step in the future. Willie chuckled, savoring his moment of triumph in advance. He checked the angle of the sun and went back for his shovel to dig the last posthole. He could finish that and still get back in time to see the action.

The hole dug, he slipped up behind the woodshed and hid in the shelter of its walls. They should be along any minute. He strained to pick up the first indication of footsteps. He didn't plan to make a move until he heard the splash. It wouldn't do to give his position away and alert his target.

There they came, right on time. Willie grinned and prepared to enjoy his victory. The steps quickened, then paused. A slight creak from the door and then. . . *Clang!* A muffled shriek followed.

Willie leaped out from his hiding place, ready to whoop with laughter at the sight of three dripping children. Instead, he beheld a lone figure standing stock still in the henhouse doorway, an inverted bucket covering its head, and realized with a feeling of doom that he'd managed to catch Violet in his trap.

Before his horrified gaze, she staggered around in a tiny circle, arms flailing. His jaw sagged, and a jumble of bewildered thoughts whirled through his brain. Thank goodness he'd picked out the lightest bucket he could find. But where were the kids? He looked around for some sign of the Wingates, but they were nowhere to be seen.

He needed to get a towel, something to dry Violet off. He started toward the house, then stopped, struck by a peculiarity that had escaped his notice until that moment. Violet hadn't gotten a bit wet. How could that be? Maybe the water had spilled before the bucket came tumbling down upon her? A quick glance showed no puddle, no splash, no sign of water anywhere.

Mystified, Willie moved to help, but Violet tugged the bucket off before he could reach her. He skidded to a halt, stricken by the sight that met his eyes. Instead of water, a gummy substance coated Violet's head. With agonizingly slow movement, globs of the amber stuff rolled from her forehead to her nose to her chin. More oozed its way down the length of her hair. Her eyes gaped wide. Her mouth opened and closed, but she made no sound.

Willie stared, completely baffled. No water in the world looked or acted like this stuff. What on earth had happened? He sniffed, trying to place the heavy smell that emanated from Violet.

No, it couldn't be. He reached out and touched her shoulder with a tentative finger, picked up a drop of the treacly goo, and touched it to his tongue.

Molasses? Another taste convinced him.

Violet turned a stunned face toward him. "What. . .? How. . .?"

"I don't know," Willie said. "It was supposed to be water."

Violet's features froze. She narrowed her eyes into angry blue slits. "What do you mean, 'it was supposed to be water?' "

"That's what I put in the bucket," he began, then stopped, aghast, when he realized his error.

"You set this up? *You?*" Violet's chest heaved with the force of her emotion.

"Not exactly," he sputtered. "Well, sort of. But it wasn't meant for you."

Violet tried to wipe the molasses from her eyebrows, but only succeeded in stringing more of the syrup from forehead to fingers. "Then who?" She glared at Willie, targeting him with a gaze capable of freezing a waterfall. Without giving him time to answer, she went on. "The children were supposed to gather eggs. You knew that. You intended this for them, didn't you?"

She turned on her heel and stomped across the yard toward the house, radiating outraged fury. "You would have gotten them with your nasty trick, too, if Toby hadn't hurt his knee. Jessie and Frederick are helping him into bed, so I told them I'd come down here in their place."

"Wait a minute." Willie's suspicions flared to a high level. He had never yet seen a Wingate do anything without some purpose. "When did Toby get hurt? Is he bleeding?"

"It happened just a few minutes ago, and no, his knee is not bleeding. Does that disappoint you?" The sarcasm dripped more freely than the molasses.

"I just meant. . .well, if he only *said* he'd been hurt, it would be a way to keep them all in the house and make sure you came down here instead." His voice trailed off at the look of contempt she shot at him.

"Are you implying. . . ?" She shook her head, flinging molasses onto the ground. "Save your breath, Willie Bradley. It's bad enough you set up something like this without trying to cast the blame on three innocent children."

"Innocent! Compared to those three, a rattlesnake looks like a housepet."

"How can you even think of saying such a thing when you've already admitted you're the one responsible for this? Why, if I hadn't come down here, that bucket would have fallen on one of them. Which is exactly what you intended," she added with a dark look.

Willie raised his arms in protest, then dropped them, admitting defeat. "It was only water," he mumbled.

"Oh, really?" Violet fumed. "And which well did this particular water come from?" She pivoted and swept up the porch steps, leaving only a trail of molasses droplets to mark her passing.

෨

Violet lathered her hair for the third time, probing with her fingers to make sure she'd finally gotten rid of the last traces of molasses. When she encountered no more of the sticky syrup, she reached for the pitcher of rinse water.

"Violet, are you all right?" Rachel's concerned voice came from behind her.

Unable to talk without getting a mouthful of water, Violet contented herself with an affirmative grunt.

"But why are you washing your hair this time of day? And why is your dress all balled up in the corner like that?"

Violet squeezed the water from her hair, caught it up in a towel, and stood to face her sister. "I got something on my dress," she said, hoping Rachel wouldn't press for details. "And my hair." *And my face, and my ears, and my hands.*

Rachel knelt before the wadded dress. "I'll say you got something on it. Let's just hope it isn't a total loss. What on earth is it anyway?" She poked at the garment with an inquiring finger. "Why, it almost looks like. . . Violet Canfield, how did you manage to get molasses all over your head?"

"I don't want to talk about it." Violet toweled her hair vigorously, then pulled on a clean dress. "Leave it," she said, when Rachel would have picked up the soiled one. "I'll take care of it myself." She thinned her lips into a hard, straight line.

Rachel opened her mouth as if to argue, then appeared to reconsider. "All right, Honey. Have it your own way." She paused at the bedroom doorway for one last look at the puzzling sight and then left.

Violet wadded the towel into a ball and flung it next to the molasses-coated dress. She could hear Rachel's footsteps moving around in the kitchen. Apparently her sister had decided to take care of the supper preparations. Good. It would give her time to think about what had happened.

The moment the bucket had toppled onto her head, she'd shrieked in alarm. That first instant of shock, though, didn't begin to compare with her feelings when something thick and heavy began to spread its way over her head and face. If she hadn't managed to pull the bucket free and regain contact with her surroundings, she knew she would have dissolved into hysterics. The memory still left her shaken.

And then to find Willie right on the scene telling her she'd been covered in molasses. Molasses, of all things! His look of assumed innocence had been so well contrived she almost would have believed him blameless, if he hadn't admitted his guilt in setting up the trap. Why he insisted he'd only filled the bucket with water was something she couldn't understand. A forthright confession and apology would have gone a long way toward mollifying her feelings. Maybe when he realized the enormity of what he'd done, he'd been afraid of what she might do.

And well he should be! Violet couldn't ever remember being so utterly furious in her entire life. In any case, Willie Bradley had shown his true colors at last. Sir Willie? Ha! More like the Black Knight. She paced the width of the room, the staccato beat of her footsteps punctuating her angry thoughts.

Hadn't she given him every opportunity to prove her first impression of him wrong? He'd done a good job of pulling the wool over her eyes too. Her cheeks flamed when she remembered her tender response to the way he'd ridden off to fetch Doc Hathaway, the joy she felt when their eyes met and his smile lit up his suntanned face. She'd even begun to wonder if. . .

No. She must thrust away such foolish thoughts. It turned out her first assessment had been the right one all along, and she had to face the fact. No matter what she'd thought—what she'd hoped—might be true, today's episode only proved the children's stories correct. The man simply couldn't be trusted.

It shouldn't be difficult to come to terms with that. Why, then, did the thought leave her feeling so bereft? She'd lived a peaceful, happy existence before he barreled into her life. She could go back to that placid, dreamy state when he left. After all, he'd made it all too clear he wanted nothing more than to go his way as soon as possible ever since he arrived.

All right, then. He would be out of her life before much longer. His character, however deplorable it might be, shouldn't bother her in the least. She touched her hand to her cheek and stared at the traces of wetness on her fingertips. And thoughts of his departure surely shouldn't make her cry.

fifteen

"I'm taking this load of corn over to Zeke Thomas's." Daniel stepped up into the wagon seat and picked up the reins. "I may not be back until suppertime."

"Want me to take it for you?" Willie hoped his eagerness to get off the place didn't show.

Daniel sent him an appraising glance that told him his hope had been in vain. "It's been pretty rough on you the past few days, hasn't it?" A grin crinkled the corners of his eyes. "I've heard your version and I've heard Violet's, and I'm still not sure what to make of what happened. Whatever it was, I wish I'd been there." He leaned back and slapped his thigh. "I don't think I've ever seen Violet as stirred up over anything. It must have been a sight to see."

"Oh, it was. Believe me."

Daniel chuckled at Willie's dry tone and jumped down from the seat. "Go ahead. The time away should do you good." He clapped Willie on the back and walked toward the barn, still laughing.

Wish I could see it in the same light Daniel does. Willie guided the horses onto the road to Thomas's place and tried to get his mind to think of happier things than Violet's attitude of late. Every time he came within twenty feet of her, she sniffed and left in a pointed manner that made it clear he was the reason for her departure.

He'd tried more than once to explain to her, but she refused to stay around long enough to listen. He thought about confronting the kids and forcing them to confess their part in the fiasco, but Violet kept them firmly out of his sight. He sighed. What could a fellow do? *Go away and leave her in peace, I reckon.*

And so he would. . . just as soon as he found Thurman Had-lock. The gloomy thought did nothing to brighten his spirits. He unloaded the corn for Zeke with barely a word of greeting and left the puzzled man scratching his head.

He glanced at the sun. It hadn't taken nearly as long as he thought it would. At this rate, he'd be home well before sup-pertime. He hauled back on the reins, bringing the surprised horses to a halt in the middle of the road.

He needed time away, and Daniel wouldn't expect him for several more hours. He clucked to the horses and wheeled them around in the opposite direction. For the first time since he arrived, he had the opportunity to see more of the area than the farm and the road into town. He would do a little exploring.

He paused a moment to get his bearings. To reach Zeke Thomas's place, he'd crossed a ridge about two miles east of the farm, which put him on the northeast side of Granite Mountain. Willie nodded. The craggy peak that loomed above him made an easy reference point. He snapped the reins and started the horses again.

The road meandered through broad open areas and under stands of pine trees. He filled his lungs with their pungent scent, glad he had chosen this course. For one who'd spent most of his life crossing the range on horseback, the past weeks had been unbearably confining. He'd needed this change of scene.

He stopped the wagon at the edge of a smooth, rolling meadow and set the brake. The sun sent warm beams down from an azure sky as clear as any he'd ever seen at home. Leaving the horses where they could reach the new spring growth, Willie walked across the springy meadow grass. He tried to name the trees he saw scattered throughout the expanse: cottonwoods, walnuts, and some good-sized oaks.

Once he left the meadow and entered the trees on the other side, a thick layer of leaves and pine needles cushioned his steps. He stopped at the foot of a towering pine and settled himself against its trunk. What a view! A tree-studded foothill behind him, the rolling grassland before him—what more could a man ask for?

He perused the area with an experienced eye. The winter must have brought plenty of moisture; he could tell from the new growth that lush graze would soon spring up. Would it be like that every year? If so, wouldn't this be the perfect setting for a ranch?

He grinned at his foolish notion. Making himself more comfortable on the pine needles, he rested his arms on his knees and let the quiet of the place seep into his soul. After listening to the kids' chatter for weeks on end and spending every moment he could in search of Hadlock, this quiet spot seemed like a piece of heaven. Apart from the sound of the wind soughing through the trees, nothing reached his ears but the horses' steady munching.

"You like this place as much as I do, don't you, fellas?"

A flicker of movement caught his attention and he spotted a gray, bushy tail just before it disappeared behind the trunk of a nearby pine. The squirrel peeked out from the other side and chittered at him. "But you found it first and you wish we'd get on our way, is that it?" He laughed and folded his arms behind his head. What made this place so special? Peace, he decided.

What a man could do here! He scanned the setting before him. Up on that ridge would be a perfect setting for a house. Right near those massive pines, sentinels of the forest. Then, noticing the bright stripe that spiraled down the trunk of one of them, he revised his opinion. Maybe not. It wouldn't do to build anywhere near the likelihood of another lightning strike.

He shifted his position and kept looking. All right, what about down in that sheltered hollow? It still commanded quite a view. Yes, that would work. He turned his attention to the broad expanse opposite it. In his mind's eye, he could see tawny cattle hides dotting the landscape, moving through clumps of manzanita and cliff rose.

Scooting into a reclining position, he tilted his hat low over half-closed eyes and went deeper into his pleasant daydream.

The corrals would go. . .over there, he decided. The barn would be placed nearby. Both would be only a reasonable walking distance from the house. It wouldn't be a fine house like his parents' or his uncle's—not at first anyway. But he could start out small and build on as necessity demanded. In his mind, he mounted the steps to the porch. The door opened.

Willie's lips curved upward, wondering who would appear. He tried to insert Mary Rose Downey into his mental picture, but her image faded as quickly as it appeared. Mary Rose would never be suited for a life away from boardwalks and town amenities. Ranch life needed to be lived by someone like. . .Violet.

Violet? The notion made him start bolt upright, then sink back to his more relaxed position. He had to admit it: Violet fit the setting as though it had been created just for her. Mary Rose's mincing city steps would never manage to cross that broad meadow without stumbling. But Violet's easy stride would move over the land with grace.

He shook his head and the picture faded. No point in entertaining any such thoughts about Violet Canfield. The woman despised him, pure and simple. He couldn't rid himself of the image of the ranch so easily. Something about the place touched a chord deep within him, one he'd known existed but had told himself he might as well ignore. Now he wondered—could the Lord have shown him the place he could claim as his own?

In a daze, he turned the horses in the direction of the farm and gave them their heads. While they plodded homeward, Willie tried to sort out the startling thoughts that clamored for attention in his mind.

❧

"Jessica?" Violet pulled her shawl tighter about her shoulders and strained her ears to hear any reply the little girl might make. Jessie usually answered quicker than her brothers. Today, though, her repeated calls brought no response.

She cast another glance at the leaden sky, and a prickle of fear ran up her arms. Surely the children wouldn't have ventured too far afield on a day like this. "Toby? Frederick?" Her voice carried clearly across the pasture. They would have heard her if they were anywhere nearby.

Worry knotted her stomach. The temperature had dropped that morning, bringing a return of crispness to the air. She hadn't been overly concerned, though, not with the children bundled up against the change in the weather. But the light clouds that dotted the morning sky had become a heavy gray mass by early afternoon; and if Violet didn't miss her guess, a storm was brewing.

If only she hadn't gotten so caught up in her spring-cleaning chores. Focused on scrubbing out cupboards and cleaning behind furniture they seldom moved, she'd lost all track of time. . .and the changing weather conditions.

She needed to locate the children, and soon. But how? She'd been calling for the last twenty minutes. She'd even rung the dinner bell, hoping that would bring the three of them scampering out of the woods that bordered the farther field. Nothing.

Rachel and Daniel would pick this day to spend the afternoon with Sheriff Dolan and his wife. If she had Daniel here, she knew he'd think of a solution. But she had only herself to rely on. Everyone else was gone. . . .

Except Willie. Violet clenched her teeth and gripped the ends of her shawl in her fists. No way did she want to make that man feel he'd somehow gotten back in her good graces. Not after what he'd done. She'd avoided him ever since the molasses incident and didn't see any reason to change that now.

Except that she didn't see any other way to find the children.

Muttering, she set off for the barn. He ought to be inside, sharpening tools.

❧

Willie looked up at the sound of footsteps, and his jaw dropped when he saw Violet standing in the doorway. He sat unmoving, not knowing what she'd come for. He didn't want to do anything to set her off again. He watched while she drew herself up and hugged herself tightly.

"I can't find the children." Her voice trembled.

He didn't know what he expected, but it hadn't been that. After keeping up her steadfast silent treatment so long, he knew she wouldn't break that silence for any trifling reason. But for the life of him, he couldn't understand what inspired such anxiety in her now. The kids had probably decided to have a little fun with her and refused to come when she called. Irritating, but not a cause for fear.

"Have you looked in the corn crib?" he asked. "What about the chicken coop or that spot over by the tree line where the boys have been playing soldier?"

"I've looked everywhere." She batted her eyelashes furiously against the brimming tears, but Willie saw how close she was to breaking down. "Have you seen what's happening outside? We're likely to be in for a storm in another hour or so, a bad one. I'm telling you, Willie, I've looked in every place I can think of, and those children are *gone.*"

Willie strode to the door, galvanized by the urgency of her tone. Sure enough, heavy gray clouds massed across the sky. The wind had picked up too. Violet was right: They needed to find those kids, and they had no time to lose.

"Show me the last place you saw them," he told her.

⁂

An hour later, Violet trotted her horse beside Willie's, nearly frantic with fear. They had checked all the children's usual haunts once more at Willie's insistence, but to no avail. Only when they made one last trek across the pasture did he notice three fresh sets of footprints leading away from the farm and into the trees.

"They've taken off," he told her, a grim set to his mouth. "I'll saddle up and go looking for them."

"I'm going with you."

"In this weather? I don't think so."

"When you find them, you'll need an extra hand to get them all home. I'm going, and that's all there is to it." She pivoted on her heel and walked to the house to get her warmest coat and extra blankets for the children when they found them. For once, he didn't argue with her.

Rather than hitch up the wagon, Willie saddled horses for them both. They'd never be able to maneuver the wagon far off the road, he explained, and no telling what kind of terrain they'd have to cross following the tracks. At first the trail seemed clear enough, at least to Willie. He followed without hesitation for nearly a mile, then shook his head.

"It seems to peter out right here in these rocks," he said. He twisted in his saddle, scanning the area on all sides, then turned to Violet. Worry puckered his forehead. "I don't understand it. How did they get this far from home in the first place, and where could they be heading?"

Violet only shook her head, unable to speak past the tears that clogged her throat. How could she have been so preoccupied as to not notice the children's disappearance? She shrugged her coat farther up around her neck. The storm would hit within the hour; she had no doubt. And when it did, what would happen to the children? Would Jessie suffer a relapse, or worse, because of her negligence?

"There are some caves up along the ridge," she managed to say. "Daniel mentioned them the other evening after supper. Maybe they decided to go explore them."

Willie touched his heels to his horse's flanks, and without hesitation her mount followed.

❧

If Willie hadn't been concerned when Violet first told him the kids had gone missing, he was now. Those gray skies spelled trouble, and three youngsters—even three as ornery as the Wingate brood—just might meet their match when pitted against the weather's fury. And now he had Violet's safety to think about as well. He couldn't believe it when she informed him she would be coming along; but after one look at her set face, he hadn't taken time to argue. He knew stubbornness when he saw it.

Where in the world could those three be? He'd hoped to find the three wanderers within a few minutes of beginning the search. By now, they must have traveled two or three miles from the farm. If the storm hit, he and Violet would have to take shelter themselves.

"Are those the caves?" He pointed to a series of pock-marked openings along a ledge of the limestone cliff. Violet nodded. They both dismounted and hurried up the slope, checking each cave in turn. No sign that the Wingates had ever been there.

"We're heading home," he said. "We can start looking again as soon as the storm has passed."

"But the children!" Violet's horrified gasp tore at his heart.

"They're either safe or they aren't. There isn't a thing we can do for them now, except pray." And he'd been doing plenty of that, ever since they started. He took long strides down the slope, sliding the last few feet to the bottom on the layer of loose rocks near the base. Behind him, he heard the rattle of rocks and a sharp cry. He turned to see Violet waving her arms wildly, trying to regain her lost footing.

He reached for her, but her feet shot out from under her before he could manage it. She slid to within six feet of him and lay there in a crumpled heap.

"Violet! Are you all right?" He cupped her face in his hands, willing her to open her eyes. In a few moments, she blinked slowly, then stared up at him.

"Are you hurt? Answer me."

Her eyes cleared and she pushed herself to a sitting position. "I'm fine. Just clumsy, I guess. I feel so foolish."

"I should have given you a hand." He berated himself for the oversight. Thank heaven she hadn't been injured. He slid his arm around her shoulders to help her to her feet. She stood, then sank back to the ground with a moan. "What is it? What's wrong?"

"It's my ankle. I must have twisted it when I fell."

Willie helped her ease off her boot. If they hadn't had trouble aplenty before, they did now. Violet's ankle had started to swell. It seemed to be increasing in size even while he watched. He sucked in his breath. Would she be up to making the ride back to the farm?

He probed the swollen flesh with gentle fingers. "How much does that hurt?"

Her low moan and ashen face gave him all the answer he needed. He didn't know whether the ankle was broken or not. He did know Violet was in no shape to be riding.

The first light splats of rain pattered down on him and he glanced up at the sky. The storm had come even more quickly than they thought. They needed to find shelter and find it fast. He wrapped his arms around Violet and lifted her up.

"I don't know how I'm going to make it home," she said in a weak voice.

"We aren't going home." He took a cautious step onto the loose rocks, looking for a foothold. "We're going up to the caves." Violet's head lolled against his shoulder with a weary acquiescence that worried him.

sixteen

The unyielding hardness of the rock beneath her brought Violet back to awareness. She pressed her hands against the floor of the cave and pushed herself upright. A hot shaft of pain stabbed her ankle, and she cried out.

Pulling the hem of her skirt out of the way, she tried to examine her injury. To her surprise, her ankle was encased in a neatly bound splint. When had Willie done that? She didn't remember a thing since the moment he had scooped her into his arms and carried her back up the hill.

More to the point, where was Willie now? She swiveled her head back and forth, peering into the recesses of the cave's dim interior. She couldn't see him anywhere. Outside, the sky had unleashed a deluge of rain. What trees she could see through the darkness of the storm bent like buggy whips in the wind.

Where is he? Surely he wouldn't have gone off and left her! Panic at the thought of being alone and injured welled up inside her and threatened to overflow in a torrent of fear.

Footsteps rattled against the stones just outside the mouth of the cave. Violet bit her lip to keep back the tears of relief that sprang to her eyes. In a moment Willie appeared, swathed in a dripping slicker and staggering under the weight of their saddles, blankets, and saddlebags. "There, that ought to do it." He dropped the blankets and saddles near a pile of dry pine branches and slung the saddlebags over near the rock wall.

"Where have you been?" She hadn't meant for the question to come out in a high-pitched squeak.

Willie looked at her, compassion and amusement mingled in his gaze. "I had to get things squared away before I could come back and hole up here. This isn't any too big," he said, waving his hand at their small shelter, "but anything much larger would be too hard to heat."

He shucked off his slicker and began laying a fire at the mouth of the cave. "I put the horses in the next one over," he went on. "They should be fine. I have some jerky in my saddle-bags and water in my canteen. We're in pretty good shape." He lit the kindling and blew the small flame to life.

"You call this good?" Violet wrapped her arms around herself and tried to keep from shivering.

"It could be a lot worse. We have shelter, food, and fire. We'll be fine." He added more wood to the growing blaze, then came to sit next to her. "How's your ankle?"

"It hurts," she admitted. Then, remembering the splint, she added, "Thank you for binding it up for me. Do you think it's broken?"

"I couldn't tell for sure. We'll take another look at it in the morning. You look like you're feeling a little better now. I'm glad." He gave her a gaze that rivaled the fire for its warmth.

Violet felt her cheeks flush. "I feel fine, except for my ankle." And the way she went lightheaded when he looked at her like that. "Willie. . .do you think the children are all right?"

The crease that furrowed his brow told her he'd wondered that himself. "I think so. I hope so. They're young, but they're all smart kids. They might not have known about the storm ahead of time, but once it got close, I bet they figured out a place to take shelter, just like we did."

She wanted to believe him, *needed* to hold on to his comforting words.

❧

The rain continued unabated. Willie stoked the fire yet again, then leaned back against the cave wall. In their small quarters, the modest blaze threw off enough heat to keep them from freezing without requiring too much of the wood he'd gathered earlier. Light from the fire flickered around the cave, throwing shadows into weird, dancing patterns on the walls.

He looked at Violet and saw her shiver despite the blanket

he had wrapped around her hours before. He scooted closer to her and pulled the sleeping woman into his arms.

"What? Hmm?"

"Shhh. Just be quiet." He stroked her hair, smoothing loose tendrils back from her forehead. She murmured once more, then relaxed back into slumber. Willie shifted his position slightly and settled back against the wall again. Their shared body heat should help keep them both warm until morning. It wouldn't do to let Violet get sick on top of everything else.

That look on her face when she came plummeting down the slope had scared him more than he wanted to admit. That, and the way she had sagged against him, uncomplaining, when he carried her uphill. Coming back into the cave to find her sitting up and back to her old self made him want to shout with gratitude, but he contained his joy and made himself continue with his preparations for the night without comment.

Violet's injured foot had come out from beneath her blanket when he moved her, and he leaned over to cover it again. He squinted at her ankle in the firelight. Had the swelling gone down slightly? Hard to tell with the splint strapped to it. He tossed the corner of the blanket over it and gathered Violet closer to him.

Her warmth penetrated both his body and his heart, and he allowed himself to savor her nearness. *It feels right to hold her in my arms, Lord. How am I supposed to keep my distance after this?* But keep it he would. He couldn't inflict his presence on her any longer than necessary, knowing all he'd brought her had been misery, hard work, and pain.

And a passel of kids for her to love. The thought came unbidden to his mind, and he wondered for the thousandth time whether the trio had made it to some place of protection. Despite his calming words to Violet, he didn't know whether they'd have sense enough to realize the coming danger or not. And he knew they didn't have the wherewithal to light a fire. Would three small bodies huddling together be able to keep each other warm on a night like this?

Only time would tell. Tomorrow he would manage somehow to get Violet back to the farm. Then he'd round up every able-bodied man he could and comb the forest until those kids were found.

He turned his attention back to the woman in his arms and smiled when she murmured in her sleep. The constant downpour outside lulled him into drowsiness, and he let his eyelids drift closed. Immediately, he opened them again. He might never again have the opportunity to hold Violet Canfield close to him. He wanted to stay awake and enjoy the moment while it lasted.

He sat staring into the fire, holding his welcome burden and listening to the sound of the rain. It slackened by degrees, then slowed to a mere drizzle. Willie heaved a sigh. By all appearances, it would let up by morning. They would be able to get back home. The weariness he had tried to hold at bay overcame him. Despite his best intentions, he slept.

≈

Violet floated in a beautiful dream in which she and Willie shared a meal before a cozy fireplace. The corners of his eyes crinkled with laughter, and he smiled at her as though there had never been any rift between them. In his blue gaze she saw an intensity that matched her own feelings, a look that hinted at something far deeper than friendship. He leaned toward her and. . .

Something shifted behind her. Strong arms moved her gently to one side. "Something's bothering the horses," Willie whispered. "I've got to go check on them." He took two quick strides to the mouth of the cave and disappeared along the ledge.

She fought to bring herself completely awake. Willie had gone to see to the horses. That made sense. But had his arms been wrapped around her, or had she confused that with her dream? And had she imagined it, or had he really dropped a gentle kiss on her temple just before he left?

She pulled the blanket back around herself and stared out into the gray dawn. The rain had finally ended. Good. There would be nothing to stop them from going home at first light and organizing a search for the children. With some misgivings, she tried rolling her foot from side to side and felt a thrill of hope when it didn't respond with the shooting pain of the day before. Maybe it wasn't broken after all.

Willie's boots scraped along the ledge, and he poked his head inside the opening. "They're all stirred up about something," he told her, "but I can't figure out what it is. I'll circle around up above the caves and be right back."

She nodded, her mind already busy planning what they should do first on their return. She scooted her way across the floor and poked another stick into the fire, not wanting to lose any of its warmth until they were ready to leave.

High-pitched whinnies sounded from the next cave, followed by the stamping of nervous hooves. Violet frowned. Normally, the horses didn't act like that unless they felt in danger. What could be bothering them so? She squinted out into the morning, hoping Willie hadn't come to any harm, and saw a tawny paw at the edge of the opening.

Her breath caught in her throat, and she watched in horror as another paw appeared beside the first and the mountain lion's face moved into view just outside the cave. The creature seemed to take notice of her at the same instant. For an endless moment, their gazes locked. Then the big cat's lips drew back in a snarl and its muscles tensed.

Violet grasped the cool end of the stick she had just added to the fire and waved its blazing end at the cougar. The movement knocked her off balance and she fell to one side. With her ankle in its splint, she couldn't hope to rise to her feet. All she could do was wriggle along on her side, continuing to brandish her improvised torch in the face of the snarling animal.

The mountain lion made a tentative swat toward her with one paw. Violet's heart pounded. If the beast chose to attack her, she could do nothing more to defend herself. The cat, seeming to understand it faced a helpless prey, crouched back on its haunches and waited for the opportunity to spring.

Yaaaahh! A shout echoed through the morning air, and Willie appeared to drop straight from the sky, landing on the ledge not ten feet from the menacing animal.

The cat twisted its body to face this new foe in one lithe movement, muscles rippling along its glossy hide. No sooner had Willie landed than a shot rang out. The cat leaped into the air, then disappeared in a tawny blur.

For a moment, neither of them moved. Violet was the first to find her voice. "Did you get it?" she asked through trembling lips.

Willie shook his head. "I shot too fast. I saw it streaking off through those trees up there." He dropped to one knee beside Violet. "Are you all right?"

"I am now." She regained a sitting position. "I never heard anything more wonderful in my life than that yell you gave a moment ago."

Willie's laugh sounded a bit shaky. "I'd spotted some sign higher up the hill. I was just coming back to tell you when I saw the lion outside our cave and you flailing at it with that burning branch." He cupped her cheek with one hand. "You are one plucky woman, Violet Canfield."

Violet closed her eyes and leaned into his touch. If he hadn't gotten there when he did. . . She opened her eyes and looked up at him. The force of his gaze rocked her. Neither of them moved; neither of them spoke.

Willie was the first to break the silence. "We'd better go," he said, pulling his hand away. "No telling how far that cat went or how long he'll stay gone."

❧

The horses picked their way, trying to find the firmest footing on the slick, muddy ground. Willie kept his attention fixed on the path before him, wanting to spot any potential trouble spots before they could cause a problem. They'd had disasters enough in the past day without adding any more.

Three lost kids, an injured woman, a night stranded in a cave, and an encounter with a cougar. He shook his head and shot a quick glance toward Violet to see how she was faring. She seemed to be holding up well, despite having to keep weight off her ankle. If she could manage to sit her horse for another mile, they'd be home.

And then they could explain to Daniel and Rachel why no one had been home when they came back from town yesterday. His stomach tightened at the thought. Couldn't he last a week without bringing some fresh calamity upon this family? They'd be as glad to see the last of him as he would be to finish his responsibilities to the Wingates and get out of there.

His mood darkened like the previous day's sky. If he had come out to Arizona with any notion of proving himself, he had been sadly mistaken. Not only couldn't he find the kids' guardian; at the moment he had no idea where the kids themselves might be or what condition they were in. He recalled his father's trust in him when he placed them in his care, and his outlook soured even further. It seemed he couldn't do anything right. *So much for being a hero.*

* * *

Violet gave her horse its head, trusting the surefooted animal to follow Willie's lead. Clinging to the saddle horn with both hands, she concentrated on keeping her weight shifted away from her injured ankle. Pictures of their ordeal on the mountain flashed through her mind nonstop: her fall down the slope, Willie's quick response to their predicament, the miserable night in the cave, the heart-stopping moment when she'd locked eyes with that mountain lion, and Willie's amazing appearance out of thin air to drive the beast away.

It had taken a day of such extremes to open her eyes to the truth about Willie. When faced with an impossible task, he'd forged ahead without complaint. The moment she'd asked him for help, he'd come to her aid without hesitation, despite her previous cold treatment of him. He never upbraided her for her carelessness in losing her footing and stranding them in the downpour. And never once had he treated her with anything but the utmost courtesy and concern.

How had she failed to recognize a real-life champion from the first? The irony of the situation struck her with a bitter pang. She'd met the hero of her dreams at last and nothing could possibly come of it. How could she bring herself to tell him of her feelings, knowing how much he wanted to leave?

seventeen

The front door flew open by the time they'd reached the gate, and both Daniel and Rachel hurried across the yard to meet them.

"Are you all right?"

"We've been so worried."

"What on earth possessed you to take off in weather like that?"

Questions and demands for explanation tumbled over one another. Willie waited until they had run down, then held up his hand. "First off, let's get Violet onto the porch. She needs to prop up her ankle."

Rachel gave a muffled cry of dismay and stepped back to let him carry her sister up the stairs and settle her in one of the rocking chairs. She fetched a stool and helped Violet ease her foot onto it. "Is it broken?" she asked when she saw the splint.

"I don't think so," Violet replied. "It feels much better than it did yesterday. Willie took very good care of it." The smile she sent his way did a lot toward bolstering him for the ordeal of telling the others about losing the kids and the need to organize a search party.

He braced himself against the porch railing and faced Daniel. "We have to make some plans. I don't know how to tell you this—"

"We already know." Daniel gave him a solemn nod. "Although I must say, I wish you'd waited long enough to tell us yourself. We were only in town for the day, after all."

Willie exchanged a puzzled look with Violet. Obviously they knew the children weren't there, but how could they have learned the reason? And why would they have expected Willie and Violet to wait any longer to start their search with

147

that storm headed their way? He looked at Daniel for some clue as to the man's reasoning but couldn't read his expression. "We didn't have time," he said, feeling the other's disapproval even as he spoke.

Rachel stepped toward her sister with an exasperated sigh. "Honestly, Violet, this is really too much. I know Daniel and I had our wedding only a week after he proposed, but at least we let people know and took the time to do it right."

Violet's bewildered expression matched the way Willie felt. He held up both hands and took a deep breath. "Would someone please explain what's going on?" He hadn't meant for the statement to come out as loudly as that, but it had the desired effect. Everyone on the porch focused their attention on him. "We're trying to tell you why we've been gone all night," he began.

"But we already know why," Rachel responded. "The children told us."

Willie gaped. "The kids? You mean they're here?"

Daniel nodded slowly, looking at Willie as though he thought he'd lost his mind. "They got home just before we did. The little scamps had taken off on a hike and gotten as far as Jeb McCurdy's place. He bundled them up in his wagon and brought them home just before the storm hit. Good thing he did, too. It wouldn't have been any fun to be caught out in weather like that."

Willie knew that only too well. He calculated for a moment. That meant everyone had been converging on the farm just about the time Violet had hurt her ankle. That meant. . .

"They've been here all the time?" he asked in a hollow voice.

"Except for when they went off to play after you left," Rachel told him. "And I must say I'm surprised at you both for doing that. I know you expected us home fairly soon, but to leave those little things on their own just so you could run off—"

"Run off?" Willie and Violet asked in unison.

"—to get married. Really, don't you think you could have

waited just a bit, even if you felt you had to elope?"

A gray mist swirled in front of Willie's eyes. He waited to speak until he could blink it away. "Let me get this straight. The kids have been here—safe—all this time? And they told you we had eloped?"

Daniel hooked his thumbs in his pockets and nodded. "That's about the size of it."

"But that's not true!" Violet's anguished cry rang out. "They ran off and we thought they were lost in the storm. We went out looking for them, and when I hurt my ankle, we were stranded overnight." Willie noted the look of horror filling Violet's eyes as she sought out Rachel. "They really said that?" Violet asked in a stunned whisper.

"They really did." Daniel answered for his wife, his lips set in a grim line. He turned to Willie. "I think we owe you an apology. Looks like we should have listened more carefully when you tried to tell us about some of the things they've pulled."

A week ago, Willie would have found immense consolation in this statement. Today any satisfaction he might feel at this vindication paled beside Violet's obvious misery. He watched her features crumple before she buried her face in her hands. When Rachel tried to comfort her, she shook her head. "Would everybody please leave me alone?" The words came out muffled, but their meaning was clear: Once again, Violet wanted no part of him.

❧

Footsteps scraped on the wooden porch, first shuffling uncertainly, then receding. Violet listened to the soft click when the front door closed behind Rachel and Daniel and heard Willie's steps stride away across the packed dirt toward the barn. She pressed her hands still tighter against her eyes, wishing she could somehow disappear into the comforting darkness and never have to face any of them again.

What must Daniel and Rachel have gone through, thinking she had run off to marry Willie? Her spirit writhed in mortification. How could they have believed such a story? *The same way you believed every awful thing the children told you about Willie.* Those sweet faces seemed incapable of housing such devious minds. He had tried to tell her over and over, but she'd refused to listen to anything that might contradict her perception of them. A fresh spasm of agony pierced her when she thought how much Willie must have suffered.

How could she have misjudged them all? Willie had shown himself to be the kind of man she always dreamed of, while the children. . . Violet thought back to their times together: stories they'd read, games they'd played, the awful period of nursing Jessie back to health. In all that time, she hadn't once seen anything to give her the slightest qualm. Would she be able to go on caring for them after this?

After a moment's thought, she knew she would. Her love for them had grown so deep, she couldn't cut it off like the flow of water from a pump. *Is this how God feels when we hurt Him and He goes on loving us just the same?* She reflected on the number of times she'd carelessly taken His love for granted. Never again would she do so, now that she had some idea of the cost.

She pulled her hands away from her face and wiped the dampness on her skirt. She stared across the pasture, where Willie had started to work setting a new fencepost. Had she learned anything from this awful episode? Undoubtedly. She, Violet Canfield, was a terrible judge of character. She noted the strength in Willie's arms when he lifted the post into place. Those same arms had held her, given her comfort and warmth all through the night. They belonged to a good man, one to whom she feared she had already given her heart.

With a low cry, she covered her face again, trying to erase the memory of the joy she had felt in Willie's arms, and the kiss—real or imagined—he had pressed against her forehead in the night.

❧

"They did *what?*" Sheriff John Dolan pushed his hat back on his head and stared at Willie with round eyes.

Willie continued filling him in on his and Violet's supposed elopement. When he finished, Dolan puffed out his cheeks and let out a long sigh. "They're really something, aren't they? Somebody better get them straightened out before it's too late."

"I couldn't agree more," Willie said with fervor. "The sooner I find Hadlock, the better I'll like it."

"Mm." The sheriff rose from his seat on the edge of his desk and put his hand on Willie's shoulder. "I've got something to tell you. Hadlock won't be raising those kids."

"What?"

"I got into a conversation with Evan Mills yesterday. He'd just come back from San Francisco, so I asked him if he'd seen Hadlock there. Thought I'd help you out a bit if I could."

Willie nodded and waited for the blow to fall.

"Hadlock's dead. To quote Evan, 'He'd been out debauching all night and fell down a flight of stairs when he tried to go up to his room. Broke his fool, drunken neck, and good riddance.'" The sheriff gave Willie's shoulder a sympathetic squeeze and dropped his hand to his side. Eyeing Willie steadily, he asked, "What are you going to do now?"

"I have no idea." Willie tried to assimilate the news, but all he could think of was that his weeks of hard work had gone for naught. "Guess I'll wire home and see what my cousin has to say." He picked up his hat with a shaking hand and walked out the door.

"I'll be praying, Son." Dolan's words followed after him.

It took him a good while to frame a coherent message at the telegraph office. Once the wire had been sent, he felt at loose ends and decided to pick up supplies while he was in town. Daniel's new order of seeds should be in, and maybe the time spent doing something productive would help to clear his mind. He had gone a block toward the general store when he felt a hand on his arm.

"Willie Bradley, have you gone deaf? I've been calling and

calling, but you just kept walking." Mary Rose Downey looked up at him with those grass-green eyes of hers. She pushed out her lower lip in a tiny pout. "It's been ages since I've seen you," she said, circling his arm with both hands. "Come have a cup of tea with me so we can catch up."

"Not today, Mary Rose. It isn't a good time." He extricated his arm and started to walk away, hoping she'd let it go at that.

Instead, she quickened her steps and planted herself in his path. "Just what is going on? Do you think you can pay attention to me one minute and ignore me the next? I won't be treated in such a way!" A dangerous emerald gleam glowed deep within her eyes, and her lips curved up in a feline smile. "It's Violet, isn't it? You prefer that insipid little farm girl to me. Well, fine, Mr. Bradley. If you want her, you can have her." With a toss of her head, she was gone.

Willie stared after her. How had he ever considered her attractive? Memories of his mother's comments about beauty being only skin deep returned in snatches. She sure had that figured out. Mary Rose's allure didn't extend one bit beneath the surface of her pretty features. What would his mother think about Violet? He smiled, remembering her glossy sable hair and startling blue eyes and going beyond that to her ready smile, her loving heart, and the faith rooted deep within her soul. No doubt about it. Violet was beautiful, inside and out.

Two hours later, his errands completed, he stepped up into the wagon. He had just taken up the reins when he heard a voice calling his name. He turned to see the clerk from the telegraph office running along the boardwalk.

"Mr. Bradley! Glad I recognized your wagon." The man clutched the off wheel and gasped for breath. "These just came for you," he said, handing over two telegrams. "I thought you might need to know about them at once, seeing as they arrived so quickly after you sent your last message."

Willie tried to hide his astonishment long enough to thank the man and drove a little way out of town before he stopped to open the wires. Could he really have received a response in such a short time? Apparently so, but why two of them? His heart filled with misgivings, he opened the first.

> *William Adam McKenzie born May eighth STOP*
> *Mother and baby fine STOP*
> *Father insufferable STOP*
> *Pa*

He took advantage of his isolation to let out a joyous whoop. So Lizzie'd had her baby, had she? He scanned the message again, letting the first sentence sink in and register. William Adam McKenzie? Why, they'd named the baby after him! Another whoop rent the air, and the horse twitched a curious ear at the uproar.

Willie laughed out loud. He felt reconnected with his family again, sure of his place in their affection. He gave the wire one more perusal and chuckled at the last line. From the sounds of it, Adam had taken to fatherhood with a substantial amount of pride. What he'd give to be with them right now. He set the paper aside and turned to the second telegram.

> *Bring children home STOP*
> *Lewis*

How had Monroe managed such a quick answer? He must have gone with Charles to send the wire about the baby and been on the spot when Willie's telegram arrived. Nothing else would explain it. Willie stared at the paper again.

He held in his hands the words he'd hoped to see ever since his arrival. After all the long, tormenting weeks, he'd finally gotten word to go home. He folded both wires and tucked them in his shirt pocket, waiting for the realization of his deliverance to set in. Instead, a dismal feeling settled over him like a pall. He pulled off his hat and raked his fingers through his hair, trying to understand this strange reaction. Here he'd just been given leave to go back to the ranch and get rid of the kids. He could accomplish both within the week. The whole sorry episode would finally be over. He was about to go home.

And he didn't want to.

Willie looked at the sky and gauged the sun's position. He clicked his tongue at the horse and turned it back in the direction of town. He had time enough to send one more wire.

eighteen

Willie shouldered his fencing tools and carried them back to the barn. Daniel waited for him in the shadowy interior, one arm propped on the sideboard of the wagon and a speculative glint in his gaze.

"Care to explain this?" He pulled a yellow slip of paper from his pocket and waved it gently up and down. "Rachel found it in the pocket of your shirt when she started the laundry this morning. It made us both a little curious."

Even from several feet away, Willie recognized his summons home from Monroe. "I—uh, well, the truth of the matter is that I didn't want to go." He took his time putting the tools away and waited for Daniel's response.

"Uh-huh. Any particular reason?"

Willie fumbled for an answer. "Just that. . .I found some property over on the other side of the ridge. I think it would make a fine ranch."

Daniel pursed his lips. "And you're thinking about buying it? You plan to stay around here?"

"If I can." Speaking the words aloud made the whole idea seem more plausible. Willie stood straighter. "I'd like your opinion on it, if you have the time."

"Saddle up," Daniel said. "Now's as good a time as any."

The trip by horseback took much less time than his first meandering visit in the wagon. Daniel listened while Willie pointed out the features that appealed to him: the mixture of forested and open ground, the promise of abundant graze, the building sites that stirred his imagination during his first visit. He talked about the feasibility of driving in a herd of starter stock from the Double B. When he finished, he held his breath and waited for Daniel's assessment.

"I'd say you've picked a spot about as perfect as it gets." Daniel cast an approving glance at the setting. "It has everything you need and plenty of water. And I like the site you've set on for the house. You can start off small and add on for yourself. . .and whoever you may want to share it with in the future." His shrewd look made Willie's mouth go dry.

"What about money?" The directness of the question as well as the abrupt change of subject caught Willie off guard. "How do you plan to finance this venture?"

"I haven't quite figured that out yet," he admitted. Would Daniel think him a fool for even considering a move like this without sufficient funds at his disposal?

"Then let me put forth a possibility." Daniel leaned forward and went straight to the point. "The mining I did before Rachel and I got married paid off well—very well. I've been looking for someplace to invest the money. My first thought was to put it into another mining venture. That's why we went to Tucson, to check out some properties I'd heard about. But listening to your plans makes me think I'd rather keep the money closer to home.

"What would you say to my backing you in this? It wouldn't be a gift, strictly a business arrangement. Any kind of investment is a risk, but I'd rather take a chance on you than on the hope of someone else striking it rich. I'll provide the money, but you'll run the show. I won't get in your way. What do you think?"

Willie's mind reeled. The one obstacle to fulfilling his dream had just been waved aside as though it never existed. He looked at Daniel for any sign of uncertainty, but saw only a calm confidence in the other man's gaze.

He stretched out his hand. "It's a deal."

❧

A week alone on his newly acquired property proved balm to Willie's soul. Taking advantage of Rachel's generous offer to watch the children while he got acquainted with his new place, he spent days marking off the exact sites for his barn and corrals and digging the foundation for his house.

His house. The thought filled him with such joy, he felt he could hardly bear it. This would be his place, his own to do with as he pleased. He knew he'd make mistakes, but he'd learn from them and grow, just as his father and uncle had done.

After a week, though, he'd learned something else. Whether Daniel intended to or not, his comment about having someone to share the place with had stirred another desire. Much as it meant to have the opportunity to strike out on his own, without someone to share his days with, acquiring the property would be a hollow victory. And that someone had to be Violet.

She was as present in his thoughts now as she'd been the first time he imagined her coming out of the house that would soon become a reality. She filled his days with dreams and his nights with longing. He saw her everywhere he looked, imagined her delight in the flowers that dotted the meadow and the tiny animals that scampered through the trees.

The day came when he knew he had to face the situation head-on. Life without Violet wouldn't be worth living. He put down his tools, scrubbed, and dressed in his best. Then he mounted his horse and rode back to the farm to propose.

He worked on his speech all the way through the foothills and over the ridge, wanting to get the words just right, to let her know beyond a doubt how much he loved and needed her. He rode into the farmyard, his heart pounding in his throat at the realization that he'd soon have her answer. *Let her say yes, Lord. Please let her say yes.*

Three blond heads looked up from their game on the porch when they heard him coming. Three children scuttled inside the house and closed the door behind them. *Just as well,* he thought grimly. He didn't need the kids around to twist his words and mess things up. He mounted the porch steps, slicked his hair back with both hands, and knocked on the door.

Rachel opened it, slid outside, and closed the door again. She stood facing him with a half smile. "The children said you'd come."

Willie passed his hat from one hand to the other. "I'd like to see Violet, please."

Daniel walked around the corner of the house to join them. "I saw you ride up. I need to talk to you."

"Later." Willie flushed and softened his tone. "I want to speak to Violet first."

"That's what we need to discuss." Daniel put an arm about his shoulders and led him to the edge of the porch. "Dolan rode out this morning. There's been more talk. Now the story says you have a wife back home. He thought you'd want to know."

Willie groaned. "All the more reason I need to talk to Violet. I want to tell her—"

"That's the point I'm trying to make. Violet doesn't want to see you." He listened to Willie sputter and gave him a compassionate smile. "I know you're solid. In her heart, I think Violet knows it, too, but she took this real hard. Give her some time; she'll probably come around."

Willie retraced the path he'd taken so hopefully only a short time before, trying to decide on his next move. A wife, of all things! How would he ever straighten that out with Violet, especially when she wouldn't talk to him? He brooded over her reaction. It would be natural for her to be angry at his supposed deception, but to be so upset she didn't want to see him? That didn't make sense, unless. . .

Willie wheeled his horse around and rode past the farm, into the forest beyond. He could wait there until nightfall. If Violet's behavior meant what he hoped it did, he needed to talk to her without delay. And she liked watching the stars of an evening as much as he did.

ะ∾

A light breeze played with a loose strand of Violet's hair. She tucked it back behind her ear and stepped outside the circle of light coming through the kitchen window. After being shut up inside all day, she knew she had to get some fresh air. And with Rachel, Daniel, and the children all in bed, it made a good opportunity to have a quiet moment to herself.

She moved farther away from the light, the better to watch the stars come into view. There was something peaceful about the way they kept to their courses regardless of the events being played out below them, and peace was something she needed right now. Her customary tranquility had been tested beyond endurance over the past few days. She rested her hand against the porch rail and breathed deeply of the night air.

Light footsteps mounted the steps behind her and she whirled, drawing her hands to her throat when she saw the dark form before her.

"Violet? We need to talk."

Exasperation mingled with relief when she recognized Willie's voice. "I thought Daniel told you I didn't want to see you." She moved purposefully toward the kitchen door.

Willie beat her to it in two long strides and planted his shoulder against the door, barring her way. "He did. That doesn't change a thing. You need to hear what I have to say."

Violet wrapped her arms around herself and took a slow step backward. What did he think he was doing? Should she call for help?

"You know that story about us was a pack of lies," he went on. "This one is no different. I don't have a wife back home or anywhere. Not yet, anyway." He took a step toward her, and she moved away again, coming to rest against the porch rail. He closed the gap between them and caught her shoulders in a light grasp.

"I love you, Violet Canfield. I love your spirit and your courage and that love of God that shines out from you like a beacon. I've spent the past week working on the place I've dreamed about all my life, but without you it will be empty." He tightened his hold on her shoulders and drew a long, shuddering breath. "My whole life will be empty without you. What I'm trying to say—to ask you—is, will you marry me?"

Violet closed her eyes and let the lovely words wash over her like a cleansing rain. He loved her, wanted to marry her! She longed to do nothing more than melt into his embrace and give him the answer he sought. But her self-doubt held her back. Her instincts told her Willie meant exactly what he said, but her instincts had been wrong before—so very, very wrong. She couldn't risk the heartache of saying yes now, only to find out she'd been wrong again.

Fighting the desire to fling herself into his arms, she shook her head and whispered, "I can't." She felt glad for the darkness that enveloped them. She couldn't bear to see his face reflect the hurt she had inflicted.

"Are you saying you don't love me?"

"No! It's. . .it's that story."

"But you know it's a lie."

She pressed her hands together and braced herself to deal another blow. "I asked the children. They said your mother isn't the only Mrs. Bradley at the Double B." She lifted her chin, wishing she could read the truth in his eyes. "Is there another Mrs. Bradley, Willie?"

"Well, of course there is!" he sputtered. "My aunt Judith."

His *aunt?* She hadn't considered that possibility. How could she possibly know for sure?

"Do you mean to tell me you're still listening to those kids after everything they've done? You'd trust them more than you trust me?"

She didn't have to see him to know the depth of the pain she'd caused; she could hear it in his voice. But how could she bear to give her heart, then find out she'd made the most foolish mistake of her life? Her eyes brimmed with scalding tears. "It isn't you I don't trust, Willie. It's me."

He wrapped his arms around her and held her close. "I don't know how I'm going to convince you of this, Violet, but I'll find a way. I promise you, I'll find a way."

nineteen

The next morning, Willie woke with the dawn and stretched, surprised at how comfortable his thin cot felt after a week of sleeping on the hard ground. When he left Violet last evening, he'd chosen to stay at the farm instead of returning to his property. He saw no point in trying to fix up the place while the issue with Violet remained unresolved.

After he finished the early chores, he joined the family for breakfast. Violet must have told Rachel and Daniel about his visit, for they showed no surprise when he entered the kitchen. The kids didn't say a word but kept their attention focused on their plates, something that increased his enjoyment of the meal. Violet didn't speak, either, but cast wistful looks his way that only increased his desire to prove his sincerity to her.

Rachel excused the children to go outside and helped Violet clear the table. Willie and Daniel rose to start work in the field just when Frederick bolted in the front door. "Two riders coming," he cried.

"This early in the day?" Rachel gave Daniel a worried look. All four adults joined the children on the porch and watched the riders approach.

"It's Dolan and some slicked-up fellow," Daniel said.

Willie swallowed hard. He recognized the portly form. "My cousin, Lewis Monroe."

The two men stopped at the hitching rail, Dolan dismounting in one easy motion and Monroe laboring to regain the ground without mishap. If Willie's stomach hadn't tied itself into knots, he might have enjoyed the spectacle.

"Morning," Dolan called. "I have someone here I expect you'll be happy to see. Mr. Monroe rolled in on last night's

161

stage. I told him I'd bring him out first thing this morning."

Daniel broke the collective silence. "We're pleased to meet you, Mr. Monroe." He introduced himself, Rachel, and Violet.

The lawyer acknowledged the introductions, then turned a bleak eye on Willie. "I must say I found your last telegram mystifying. After all those pleas to cut your time here short, I hardly expected to tell you to return to the ranch only to get a reply reading, 'Come get them.' "

Willie cleared his throat. "Actually, your wire said to bring the kids home. But I already am. Home, that is. I plan to stay right here."

Monroe's eyes widened, and he looked around the group for confirmation. "Then I suppose I can't count on your help on my return journey?" Willie's decisive shake of his head seemed to dishearten him. He stared at the ground for a moment, then regained some of his composure.

"I can't tell you how distressed I was to learn of the demise of Thurman Hadlock. This means I'll have to take them back East with me and start a new search, perhaps for a distant relative who'll be willing to take them in."

"Nooo!" All three Wingates joined in the chorus.

"We don't want to leave!" Frederick cried.

"We like it here," Jessica wailed.

"Yeah," Toby added. "We don't want to leave Miss Violet, or Miss Rachel, or Daniel. . .or even Willie."

Willie saw the faces of the other adults mirroring his own disbelief, especially at that last statement. He looked at Monroe, wondering how the pompous lawyer would handle this situation.

Monroe patted his forehead with his handkerchief. "Be that as it may, this is a legal matter, and I must follow legal guidelines. I have no choice but to take you with me, so you may as well go pack your things now. I've made arrangements for transportation back to the railroad, and we need to leave as soon as possible. This fruitless journey has cost me quite enough time already."

The children looked from one adult to the other for support. "You mean he's right?" Frederick asked on a quavering note. "We have to go?"

"I'm afraid so, Dear." Violet bent to wrap her arms around them all. "Go ahead inside and get started. I'll come help you in a few minutes."

Tears glistened in all three pairs of eyes when they traipsed slowly into the house.

Seemingly unaware of the emotional havoc he had wrought, Monroe patted his waistcoat and gazed about him. "I must confess this has been an interesting trip. Your part of the country is quite fascinating. A bit primitive for my taste, but still worth a brief visit."

Behind him, Dolan rolled his eyes and approached the group on the porch. "I thought you'd like to know, I finally found out who's behind those stories."

Willie jerked upright as though a lightning bolt had shot through him. "Who?" he cried hoarsely. He could feel Violet tremble beside him.

"None other than Miss Mary Rose Downey," the sheriff replied. "It seems the young lady got her nose out of joint when a certain gentleman didn't pay as much attention to her as she thought he ought to."

"Mary Rose?" Willie supposed he ought to feel shocked, but somehow the revelation didn't surprise him. It only confirmed what he'd seen in her at their last meeting. If only she had taken her venom out on him and left Violet out of it! He turned a worried glance toward Violet and blinked in surprise at the radiant look on her face.

"She started the stories? Both of them?" Her voice bubbled with laughter.

Dolan nodded. "Appears that way. I didn't expect it to make you quite that happy, though," he told her with a bemused smile.

Willie caught on to the reason for her excitement. "And if you need any further confirmation, you can get it right here," he told her. He waved a hand toward Monroe. "From an officer of the court, no less."

Violet's eyes sparkled, and she turned a glowing smile on the lawyer. "Mr. Monroe, there was a silly rumor going around about Willie having a wife back in New Mexico. That isn't true, is it?"

"Willie? Married?" Monroe burst into a hearty laugh. "Oh, my dear young lady, what a singularly preposterous idea! No, I can assure you most definitely that my young cousin here has no wife." He continued in his mirth.

Willie captured Violet's hand. "Would you join me at the other end of the porch? There's something I want to ask you."

"Miss Violet!" Toby's voice rang from inside the house.

Rachel gave her sister a little push. "I'll go help them. It sounds like you have some serious talking to do."

Violet returned the pressure of his fingers and followed him to the end of the porch. Willie took both her hands in his and caressed the backs of her fingers with his thumbs. "You heard what my cousin said. Are you sure now that I don't have a wife tucked away somewhere?"

Those amazing blue eyes looked into his with an expression of pure joy. "Yes," she said.

"You know beyond a doubt that it all came from Mary Rose's imagination?"

"Yes."

Willie drew a deep breath. "Then I want to ask you again. Violet, will you—"

"Yes!" she cried, flinging her arms around his neck.

He pulled her close and buried his face in her hair, savoring its sweet fragrance of spring air and sunshine. With one arm around her waist, he cupped her chin in his other hand and tilted her face to meet his.

The sweetness of their first kiss sent skyrockets shooting off inside his brain. Violet's arms twined even closer around his neck. *Lord, a lifetime of this won't be nearly enough.* When their lips parted at last, Violet leaned against his chest and stared into his eyes. She traced his jawline with her finger and said, "I love you, Willie Bradley, do you know that?"

He stroked her hair and nodded. "But I'll never get tired of hearing it."

Footsteps clattered on the porch, announcing the return of Rachel and the children. She looked at her sister nestled in Willie's embrace, then at Daniel. "Did I miss something?"

"Say hello to your future brother-in-law," he told her, coming to congratulate Willie with a slap on the back. "This is turning out to be quite a morning."

"My heartiest congratulations." Monroe joined them on the porch. "I'm glad to be able to offer you my very best wishes before I take my leave."

At the reminder of his cousin's mission, Willie swung his glance to the three Wingates. All three of them stood beside their valises, heads drooping, the very picture of despair. Their dismal faces tugged at his heart in spite of all they'd put him through. He wished their stay here could have ended differently.

Monroe turned to the children. "Come along," he said. "I'm sure if we put our minds to it, we can have a most enjoyable ride home." His eyes filled with doubt and he turned back to Willie. "You're sure you won't consider coming along?"

"Not a chance," Willie said and smiled down at Violet. "I have plans to make and a home to build."

Dolan cleared his throat. "Just for the record, does it have to be a relative who takes the kids?"

"Not at all," Monroe replied. "Merely someone who is willing to take on the responsibility and can provide them with a good home."

"In that case, I have an idea." Dolan stepped forward and hooked his thumbs in his belt. "My wife and I have always wanted kids, but none ever came along. After all this time wishing for a family, it would be right nice to start out with one ready made, so to speak. What do you think?"

Monroe stared at the sheriff, then darted quick glances between him and the children. "Sheriff," he intoned, "I can have the papers drawn up this afternoon." He stepped off the porch and wrung the man's hand. "God bless you, Sir."

Willie grinned at the way Dolan swiped his hand on his back pocket after their handshake.

The sheriff glanced up at Daniel. "All right if I borrow your wagon to take them home?"

"Be my guest."

"The three of you come to the barn with me, then," he told his new brood. "I'll expect you to help."

Frederick eyed him warily. "What if we don't—"

"Move!"

"Yes, Sir." The three Wingates lined up and followed Dolan to the barn like baby ducks trailing their mother.

Violet patted Willie's arm. "What just happened?" she asked, her voice full of wonder.

Willie chuckled. "I'd say the right man just took over the job. He'll be the best thing that ever happened to those kids."

"Like you're the best thing that ever happened to me?" Violet smiled and snuggled closer to him, and a light blush mantled her cheek. "Just think. Some day we'll be raising our own children."

Willie nodded in happy agreement. Then a thought struck him, and his mouth went dry. He looked at Violet. "You don't think. . . Our kids won't be anything like that, will they?"

Violet lifted her chin proudly. "Of course not," she said. "They'll be Bradleys. . .just like their father."

twenty

October 1885

Violet added one last pinecone to the arrangement on the mantel and stepped back. "What do you think?" she asked.

"I think you'd better start getting ready. Guests will be arriving anytime now. I'll be along to help you in a minute."

Violet hurried to her room. After all their preparations, she could hardly believe the moment she'd looked forward to had finally arrived. She touched the yellowed satin of the wedding dress, which hung in the corner. First her mother's, then Rachel's, and now hers.

Rachel entered. "Haven't you started yet? Honestly, Violet!"

A light tap sounded at the door. "Do you need any help?" Rachel swung the door open to admit a slender blond woman.

Before she could close it again, another voice spoke. "Is there room for us, too?" Two more women, one holding a baby, slipped inside the room and took a seat on the bed.

Violet looked at the loving faces turned her way and wondered how her cup of joy could be any more full. When Willie's family—all of them—announced their plans to attend the wedding, she'd been jittery about meeting them. Five minutes after they disembarked from their rented wagons, all her uncertainty disappeared in the flurry of loving words and warm embraces. Willie's family had become hers in a matter of moments, and they made it plain they meant to include Rachel and Daniel in the bargain as well.

"For goodness' sake, Violet, quit standing there and get dressed!" Rachel plucked at the buttons on her dress, aided by Abby's nimble hands. In short order they helped her step out of the garment and held the satin gown at the ready. Judith,

Willie's aunt, moved forward to lift the flowing folds of the skirt over her head. It settled over her in a shimmering wave.

"It's beautiful," Lizzie said from the bed, where she sat holding her five-month-old son. "I'm so glad we got to come. I couldn't stand the thought of missing out on this day." She chucked a finger under the baby's chin. "And this little guy needed to meet his uncle and his new aunt."

Violet tried to stand still and let the other women work with the tiny buttons in the back. "I don't think I've ever seen Willie smile as much as when he saw his nephew for the first time. He's one proud uncle. And I'm going to enjoy being an aunt." She cast a sly glance at Rachel. "I'm going to get lots of practice at it before long."

Rachel left the last of the buttons to Abby and Judith and sank onto the bed beside Lizzie. "After being married all this time, I can't believe it's finally going to happen." She pressed her hand against her abdomen. "I just wish I didn't feel so queasy all the time."

Lizzie laughed and patted her arm. "That happened to me at first. It'll pass, but it's no fun while it lasts. How far along are you?"

"Just a couple of months. The baby should be born about the time little William here turns a year old." She ran a gentle finger over the baby's coppery curls.

"Done." Abby stepped around in front of Violet and surveyed the effect with a satisfied nod. "You look absolutely beautiful, Dear. I'm so happy for you both."

Judith tucked a wayward wisp of Violet's hair back into place. "There. Looks to me like you're ready." She placed a spray of yellow asters in Violet's arms at the same moment a knock rattled the door. Abby went to open it.

"Is it safe to come in?" Daniel asked. At her nod, he squeezed inside the crowded room.

Charles peered around the doorway. "Why don't you women-folk come on outside and give that lovely young lady a chance to breathe?" he quipped. Abby swatted him on the arm, but followed him out along with Judith and Lizzie.

Rachel stood and pulled Violet into her arms. "You've grown into a fine young woman, Honey. Ma and Pa would both be proud." She brushed a swift kiss against her sister's cheek and hurried out to take her place among the guests.

"I guess that's our cue," Daniel said with a grin. He crooked his arm and offered it to Violet. "Are you ready?"

Violet nodded, unable to speak. How could any one person deserve the blessings being poured out on her today? No one could, she decided. No one ever did. It was God's grace, pure and simple. In a few moments she would be joined to a new family, beginning a life with the man of her dreams, and all because of God's abundant love.

She walked beside Daniel to the living room, where a crowd of guests and Bradleys filled the space to overflowing. Charles and Abby's proud faces beamed at her. Behind them stood Lizzie and her husband, Adam, then Judith and Jeff and their four children. On the other side of the room, Frederick, Jessie, and Toby Dolan stood meekly beside their new parents.

And straight ahead, Willie waited for her. The presence of everyone else in the room faded into insignificance while she walked to meet him, her gaze never leaving his face. Daniel tucked her hand into Willie's, then sat beside Rachel while the minister took up his Bible and cleared his throat.

Willie clasped her hand in his, tracing tiny circles on her fingers with his thumb while he repeated his wedding vows. In a moment it was her turn. She followed the minister's leading, speaking the words of commitment to love, honor, and obey, while her heart spoke a promise of its own.

I have learned what kind of man you are, Willie Bradley, and you're a blessing sent straight from God. With His help, I'll be the kind of wife you need, and I will never doubt you again.

The minister finished speaking. Willie looked at her expectantly. She raised her face to his and slid into his arms. When their lips met, tears of joy stung her eyes. This wasn't the storybook finish she had dreamed of; this would be better. This time the story wouldn't end.

When the kiss ended, Willie pulled her into a close embrace. She pressed her lips near his ear. "I love you," she whispered, "so very, very much."

"I love you, too, Violet Bradley," he whispered back. He turned his head and gave her a look that made her pulse race. "Cross my heart."

A Letter To Our Readers

Dear Reader:

In order that we might better contribute to your reading enjoyment, we would appreciate your taking a few minutes to respond to the following questions. We welcome your comments and read each form and letter we receive. When completed, please return to the following:

Rebecca Germany, Fiction Editor
Heartsong Presents
PO Box 719
Uhrichsville, Ohio 44683

1. Did you enjoy reading *Cross My Heart* by Carol Cox?
   ❑ Very much! I would like to see more books
      by this author!
   ❑ Moderately. I would have enjoyed it more if

   _____

   _____

   _____

2. Are you a member of **Heartsong Presents**? Yes ❑ No ❑
   If no, where did you purchase this book?_____

   _____

3. How would you rate, on a scale from 1 (poor) to 5 (superior),
   the cover design?_____

4. On a scale from 1 (poor) to 10 (superior), please rate the
   following elements.

   _____ Heroine   _____ Plot

   _____ Hero   _____ Inspirational theme

   _____ Setting   _____ Secondary characters

5. These characters were special because_____

_____

_____

6. How has this book inspired your life?_____

_____

_____

7. What settings would you like to see covered in future **Heartsong Presents** books?_____

_____

_____

8. What are some inspirational themes you would like to see treated in future books?_____

_____

_____

9. Would you be interested in reading other **Heartsong Presents** titles?   Yes ❏   No ❏

10. Please check your age range:
   ❏ Under 18   ❏ 18-24   ❏ 25-34
   ❏ 35-45   ❏ 46-55   ❏ Over 55

Name _____

Occupation _____

Address _____

City _____ State _____ Zip _____

Email _____

German Enchantment

Deep in the Black Forest of Germany a tradition begins—and continues across many generations. The "dance of love" is timed to the beat of ancient customs, and hearts are drawn to its rhythms.

Through the ages, love and faith are stirred by God's divine touch. Ancient traditions and places hold reminders of His faithfulness to all generations—and of His enduring love.

paperback, 336 pages, 5 ³⁄₁₆" x 8"

❤ ❤ ❤ ❤ ❤ ❤ ❤ ❤ ❤ ❤ ❤ ❤ ❤ ❤ ❤ ❤ ❤

❤ ❤ ❤ ❤ ❤ ❤ ❤ ❤ ❤ ❤ ❤ ❤ ❤ ❤ ❤ ❤ ❤

····Heart♥ng····

HEARTSONG PRESENTS TITLES AVAILABLE NOW:

(If ordering from this page, please remember to include it with the order form.)

Presents

Great Inspirational Romance at a Great Price!

Heartsong Presents books are inspirational romances in contemporary and historical settings, designed to give you an enjoyable, spirit-lifting reading experience. You can choose wonderfully written titles from some of today's best authors like Peggy Darty, Sally Laity, Tracie Peterson, Colleen L. Reece, Lauraine Snelling, and many others.

When ordering quantities less than twelve, above titles are $2.95 each.
Not all titles may be available at time of order.

Hearts♥ng Presents
Love Stories Are Rated G!

That's for godly, gratifying, and of course, great! If you love a thrilling love story but don't appreciate the sordidness of some popular paperback romances, **Heartsong Presents** is for you. In fact, **Heartsong Presents** is the *only inspirational romance book club* featuring love stories where Christian faith is the primary ingredient in a marriage relationship.

Sign up today to receive your first set of four never-before-published Christian romances. Send no money now; you will receive a bill with the first shipment. You may cancel at any time without obligation, and if you aren't completely satisfied with any selection, you may return the books for an immediate refund!

Imagine. . .four new romances every four weeks—two historical, two contemporary—with men and women like you who long to meet the one God has chosen as the love of their lives. . .all for the low price of $9.97 postpaid.

To join, simply complete the coupon below and mail to the address provided. **Heartsong Presents** romances are rated G for another reason: They'll arrive *Godspeed!*